## "Let's stop playing games, shall we?"

Kim broke off, shaking her head. "Either call the police, or let me go," she demanded.

"I've no intention of doing either," Ryan returned coolly. "Not, that is, unless you make the former necessary by refusing to meet my request."

He'd offered to help her escape from her predicament, but what was she going to have to do in return? He was ruthless in business, she'd heard. No doubt in private life, too. "All right," she said. "I'll listen."

"How does a trip to Canada grab you?" She stared at him wide-eyed.

"For what?"

"A spot of deception." He shook his head at the expression in her eyes. "Nothing illegal. I need someone to play the part of my wife for a short time, that's all."

**KAY THORPE**, an English author, has always been able to spin a good yarn. In fact, her teachers said she was the best storyteller in the school—particularly with excuses for being late! Kay then explored a few unsatisfactory career paths before giving rein to her imagination and hitting the jackpot with her first romance novel. After a roundabout route, she'd found her niche at last. The author is married with one son.

## Books by Kay Thorpe

# KAY THORPE

## intimate deception

**Harlequin Books**

TORONTO • NEW YORK • LONDON
AMSTERDAM • PARIS • SYDNEY • HAMBURG
STOCKHOLM • ATHENS • TOKYO • MILAN

Harlequin Presents first edition September 1991
ISBN 0-373-11397-8

Original hardcover edition published in 1990
by Mills & Boon Limited

INTIMATE DECEPTION

# CHAPTER ONE

THE sound of footsteps approaching along the corridor outside the office froze Kim's fingers on the computer keyboard for a suspended moment. Use one of the top floor offices, Tony had said; the security guard never started his rounds before eight. Trust him to get that wrong too!

A swift glance at the screen confirmed that her task was just about finished. She fed in the final hasty command, then sent the new data to the mainframe computer with a single key-press and switched off the terminal, dropping down behind the desk out of sight as the door opened. With any luck, the man would just take a quick glance round the inner office and depart. Unless he actually looked over the desk, he was unlikely to spot her.

There was no hesitation in his progress across the room. Kim steeled herself against the urge to cut and run when he entered the other office. With the door left open he would be sure to hear her, then the fat really would be in the fire. All she had to do was keep her nerve and await the right opportunity—although that in itself might not be as simple as it had first seemed if the man was varying his routine tonight of all nights.

He was certainly taking his time in there. Tony had said he was the conscientious type, but if it took him

this long to check one office he must have little rest
between rounds.

Bent beneath her, her leg was starting to cramp.
She curled the ends of her fingers around the desk
edge to ease her position, freezing once more as her
foot slipped and caught one of the supports with a
dull thud. There was sudden movement from the other
office. Kim held her breath as the man came back to
the doorway, willing him to accept the noise as a
natural settling within the building. When he spoke
it was like having a bucket of cold water thrown over
her.

'Come out of there,' he clipped.

Heart like lead, she pressed herself slowly to her
feet. Blue eyes widened as they viewed the man
standing a few feet away. This was no night-
watchman. Not unless said character earned enough
to sport Savile Row suits! Mid-thirties, at a guess, and
possessed of the kind of cool composure she would
have given her eye-teeth for at this precise moment.
The angular, uncompromisingly masculine features
were set in lines that boded ill for her immediate
future.

'You're not with Unitec,' he stated flatly. 'Who the
devil are you?'

Kim lifted slim shoulders in a resigned little shrug,
winging a mental apology in her brother's direction.
There was no way she was going to talk herself out
of this predicament; the truth was her only recourse.
Her accoster looked far from the sympathetic type,
but beggars couldn't be choosers. Perhaps he might
be prepared to turn a blind eye once he realised that
she had simply been righting a wrong.

'My name is Kimberly Anderson,' she said. 'I have a younger brother, Tony, who works in your accounts department.'

One dark eyebrow rose a fraction. 'A bit late to come looking for him, isn't it? Finishing time was more than an hour ago.'

She flushed. 'I know that. I'm just here to...help him.'

'In what capacity exactly?'

She swallowed, hardly knowing where to start. 'It's rather a long story.'

Steely grey in colour, his eyes narrowed as he studied the delicate oval of her face framed by the heavy curve of dark gold hair, moving on down the length of her slender figure and back again with a slow deliberation that brought warmth to her cheeks once more.

'Long or short, I think you'd better start telling it,' he stated. 'Come on in here.'

Kim moved forward as he stood to one side to allow her prior entry to the other office, very much aware of lean muscularity beneath the dark grey suit. The faint scent of aftershave tantalised her nostrils. Halston, if she wasn't mistaken. In high heels, she stood around five feet eight herself, but he still topped her by a good six inches. Under other circumstances, she might have found him vitally attractive; right now she could only wish herself anywhere else but here.

With only the one thought in mind, she had taken little note of her immediate surroundings over the past half-hour. Only on entering the inner office did she realise how far removed from general run of the mill they were. The whole place shouted executive suite. Her captor indicated a leather chair placed at an angle before the solid mahogany desk, leaning with his back against the latter to view her with a certain calculation.

'So?' he invited.

'Who are you exactly?' she queried, already suspecting the worst. 'Obviously someone important, if this is your office.'

The mobile left eyebrow lifted again, sardonically this time. 'Does it make any difference?'

'I don't suppose so,' she acknowledged. 'I'd just prefer to know who I'm dealing with, that's all.'

His shrug suggested barely concealed impatience. 'I'm Ryan Bentley.'

If it had been possible for her heart to sink any further, Kim was certain it would have gone right down to her feet. The company president, no less! Whatever hopes she might have entertained of appealing to the man's sympathies, they were fading fast. In his position, he was unlikely to countenance any 'softly softly' approach to what she was about to tell him.

For a wild moment she considered making up some other story to explain her presence here, but her mind refused to cope with the complexities of any such move. The truth was her only way out.

'As I said before,' she began resignedly, 'my brother works in your accounts department. A couple of weeks ago he transferred a thousand pounds to his own account in order to pay off a rather pressing debt. He always meant to repay it, of course, but the audit's being brought forward didn't give him enough time.' She wasn't looking directly at the man in front of her, but at a point somewhere in the region of his jawline, reluctant to meet the derision she could sense in the grey eyes. 'I was able to loan him the money to make restitution, but he found himself unable to make the necessary adjustments to computer records on the original transaction, when it came down to it.'

'While you obviously could.' It was a statement, not a question, the tone revealing little.

'I'm a systems programmer,' she acknowledged, still not lifting her gaze. 'I realise I'm as guilty as he is in doing this, but I couldn't just stand by and see him in trouble. Tony isn't really a bad lot, just misguided at times. I'm sure, after this scare, he'll never make the same mistake again.'

'I'm sure of it too.' There was no element of compassion in Ryan Bentley's voice. 'In order for you to log on to the mainframe, he must have supplied you with the access code—right?'

Her sigh came from way down deep. 'Yes, but——'

'There are no buts worth a penny.' He hadn't shifted his position, but his whole stance had hardened. 'Just as a matter of interest, if you're such an experienced operator, why didn't you just hack into the system here from outside—always assuming you have access to the kind of equipment you'd need.'

'I'm between jobs,' Kim confessed. 'I'm taking my holiday entitlement before I start my new job next month.'

'Choice, was it?'

The imputation was too obvious to be ignored. This time she did look him in the eyes, her own sparkling angrily. 'I wasn't fired—for any reason. The new job is a step up, both financially and in status.'

'With which company?'

She bit her lip, sensing what was coming. 'Highgate.'

A corner of the firm mouth curled a fraction. 'I think they'd better start looking again.'

'Meaning you're going to make this affair known to them?' Kim tried hard to keep her tone level. 'That's your privilege, of course.'

'Try duty,' he invited. 'I'd be neglecting it if I allowed someone capable of this kind of thing to go unchecked.' He paused, regard steady. 'Just as a matter of interest, how did you get past the security guard?'

'I came into the building earlier this afternoon and hid in a store cupboard,' she admitted.

'And how did you intend getting out again if your plan had succeeded?'

'By waiting until the guard was on his rounds then using the main door.'

'By-passing the alarm with the code also supplied by your brother, I suppose.' If the lean features had relaxed at all it wasn't noticeable. 'Give me one good reason why I shouldn't call in the police right this minute.'

'The money has been replaced,' she appealed. 'Surely that's the most important thing?'

'What's been done once can be done again,' he pointed out. 'Especially if you show your brother how to alter the records for himself.'

'I'd hardly do that!'

'Unfortunately, I don't feel able to take your word for it.'

Kim gazed at him in silence for a long, tense moment. Desperation did nothing to aid one's thought processes, she acknowledged, looking for some way out and finding none. Prosecution was sure to follow if the police were brought in, for her as well as Tony. That would mean the end of a career just beginning to get into its stride.

'Isn't there anything I can say or do that will convince you?' she pleaded. 'I know this was wrong, only I didn't want Tony to lose this job the way...'

'The way he lost others,' Ryan Bentley finished for her as she stopped and bit her lip. 'He's done the same thing before, then?'

'He's never borrowed money before.'

'The word,' he said, 'is embezzled.'

'Only if it's never paid back.'

He moved then, straightening away from the desk with an impatient gesture. 'I'm not arguing definitions with you, Miss Anderson—it is Miss, I take it?'

Kim nodded stiffly. 'For what it's worth.' She rose to her feet, steadying herself by sheer effort of will. 'If you're going to do it you'd better get it over with. I can't take any more suspense.'

He was silent for a moment, studying her, a sudden new expression coming into his eyes. When he spoke again it was on a note she found somehow more disturbing than what had gone before.

'How old are you?'

Her chin lifted. 'I don't think my age has any particular bearing.'

'It may have,' he said. 'Worth a try, at any rate.'

Anything, she thought, was worth a try, even if she couldn't see the point of the question as yet. 'Twenty-four,' she answered.

'That's pretty young to be in your position, isn't it?'

'Not really. I took my City and Guilds in programming when I was twenty, along with plenty more the same age.'

'And your brother? You said he was younger than you.'

'He's twenty-two.' It was Kim's turn to make a restless move. 'I don't really see where this is getting us.'

'I'm not all that sure myself, yet,' he acknowledged without batting an eyelid. 'Just answer the questions. What about the rest of your family?'

'My father's dead, my mother married a widower with a family of his own and lives in Australia. Tony and I share a flat in Holborn.' She trotted out the information like an automaton. 'The rent is up to date, if it's of any interest.'

'You're in no position to indulge in sarcasm,' came the unmoved response. 'Why don't you sit down again?'

'I'd rather stand, thanks.' She made no effort to keep the tartness from her voice. 'If this is just your way of keeping me on tenterhooks until you get round to picking up that phone, I'd be grateful if you'd stop it. I'll take whatever's coming to me, but for heaven's sake let's get on with it!'

Just for a moment there was a suspicion of a smile about the corners of the strong mouth. 'You don't believe in soft-pedalling, do you?' he said. 'Under other circumstances, I might even admire your spirit. Right now, it seems more than a little short-sighted.

There could be a way out of this for you. All it will take is a little . . . co-operation, shall we call it?'

Kim felt her own lip begin to curl, and not with humour. 'If you mean what I think you mean, I'd as soon take my chances with the police!'

This time the smile was more definite. 'If you mean what I think *you* mean, you're safe enough. Tempting though the thought may be, it isn't your body I have a use for at present—at least, not in any physiological sense.'

She stared at him nonplussed. 'Then what is it you *do* want?'

Broad shoulders lifted. 'This isn't the place to discuss it. Supposing we adjourn to a restaurant for dinner? You must be hungry if you've been cooped up here for several hours.'

'I don't——' She broke off, shaking her head. 'Look, let's stop playing games, shall we? Either call the police or let me go.'

'I've no intention of doing either,' he returned coolly. 'Not, that is, unless you make the former necessary by refusing what I'm going to be asking.'

'Which is what?' she demanded.

'I already said this is no place to discuss it.' He paused. 'The choice is yours.'

When it came right down to it, there was no choice to be made, Kim capitulated. Not until she had heard the proposition, anyway. What he might be going to offer her by way of escape from her present predicament, she couldn't begin to imagine. Whatever it was, the very fact that he was prepared to turn a blind eye if she agreed made him equally guilty.

'All right,' she said. 'It can't do any harm to listen.'

He turned off the lights as they left the inner office, waited for her to collect her handbag from behind the computer work-station, and opened the outer door to usher her through to the corridor. Striding at her side to the lifts at the far end, he seemed to tower. Six feet two, or even three, she thought—and every inch the dominant male! There was little use trying to get away from him when all he had to do was go through the list of company employees to find Tony. They were both in his power, and it wasn't a comforting thought.

The security guard was at his station when they reached the ground floor. He watched the two of them emerge from the lift with a look of surprise on his face.

'I didn't realise you were still here, Mr Bentley,' he said on a respectful note, and then, with a frowning glance in Kim's direction, 'I don't have anybody down as working overtime tonight either.'

'That's all right.' The younger man sounded easy. 'Miss Anderson was doing a special job for me.' He was already turning Kim in the direction of the main doors, a hand under her elbow. 'Goodnight, George.'

'He must know I'm not an employee,' Kim murmured when they were out of earshot. 'If he checks the list he'll wonder what on earth is going on.'

'If he checks the list he'll find the name Anderson under accounts personnel,' Ryan Bentley responded. 'Not that he's likely to do that anyway. With starting at six p.m., he's hardly going to know every member of staff by sight.'

'And the president himself is hardly likely to have a stranger in tow,' she tagged on with irony. 'Not unless it's a habit of yours to bring strange females into the building at night.'

Finger poised to press the key code which would turn off the alarm system for long enough to get them out of the place, he gave her an appraising glance. 'My habits aren't under review. And, while I admire spirit, I'd watch the innuendo if I were you. It still isn't too late to hand you over to the police.'

'Except that I'd be of little use to you locked up in a cell,' she pointed out, refusing to back down from confrontation with the steely gaze. 'Whatever it is you're planning on asking me to do for you, it can't be all that much above board or you wouldn't need to use blackmail!'

'True.' His control was all the more infuriating considering the sudden glint in his eyes. Kim would have given a great deal to be as capable of repression. 'Just don't make me regret it before we even get down to talking about it.'

Which left little to be said, she thought wryly, stepping outside into the chill of the December night. Tony's future, as well as her own, hinged on how she handled this man. Granted any chance at all of escaping retribution for her actions tonight, she had to take it.

A taxi had stopped along the road to drop off a passenger. Ryan Bentley hailed it, opening the rear door when it came to a halt again, and ushering Kim inside before telling the driver to take them to the Lacy's on Whitfield Street. At the very least, she reflected with faint whimsy, she was going to be eating well tonight. Whether the price would prove too much to digest remained to be seen.

There was no conversation at all during the short ride. Kim gazed out of the window at the passing scene, envying the people moving along the pavements for their very lack of involvement in this affair. Tony would be home by now, and waiting for her to confirm his release from the hook he had forged for himself, but he would simply have to wait. There was no point in getting in touch until she knew exactly where they were.

The man at her side seemed immersed in thoughts of his own. She stole a glance at the firm profile outlined against the street-lights, lingering for a brief moment on the cut of his jaw. Ruthless in business, she had heard—no doubt in private life too, where the occasion warranted it. Not a man to cross, for certain. If only she could fathom what he was up to. None of what had happened tonight could have been anticipated.

It was only just coming up to eight-thirty when they arrived at the restaurant. Apart from a few pre-theatre diners, the place had hardly begun to function. Seated in the exquisite white-vaulted dining-room, Ryan ordered drinks for them both, looking across at her with a sardonic tilt of a lip as the waiter departed.

'Are you really a sherry drinker, or out to create an impression?'

'Why should I bother pretending to be what I'm not?' Kim asked levelly. 'I happen to prefer sherry to any other pre-dinner drink, that's all.'

His glance slid over the smooth curve of her hair to dwell for a second or two on the mouth she was trying so hard to keep firm and composed. 'You don't look like a computer expert,' he commented.

'Probably because I'm not,' she responded. 'What I did tonight wasn't all that special once I knew which equipment and programs were in use.'

'Information also provided by your brother, of course.'

Blue eyes held grey. 'As a matter of fact, no. It's listed where anyone can look it up.'

'Is that so?' He sounded surprised. 'Hardly makes for good security, does it?' A movement of the broad shoulders dismissed the subject, although Kim had the feeling he would be looking into the matter a little more thoroughly, given the time. 'To get back to the main object of this exercise, how does a trip to Canada grab you?'

Sheer astonishment robbed her of the power of speech for a moment. She could only stare at him wide-eyed.

'Say something,' he invited with irony, 'even if it's only goodbye.'

'Why Canada?' she got out, and drew a sudden laugh.

'As good a place as any.'

'For what?'

'A spot of deception.' He shook his head at the expression in her eyes. 'Nothing illegal. Not that the thought should worry you. I need someone to play the part of my wife for a short time, that's all.'

'All?' It was Kim's turn to laugh, albeit on a cracked note. 'I shouldn't have thought you'd have any difficulty finding a permanent candidate for that position!'

'Probably not,' he agreed. 'Except that I've no interest in acquiring a full-time wife as yet. You said you weren't due to start your job until the New Year, which makes you available as well as suitable. Your colouring is perhaps a little darker than I had in mind, but a blue-eyed blonde covers the description well enough. You'll need some background detail, of course. That can be sorted out later.'

She said it between clenched teeth. 'Supposing you tell me exactly what it is you *do* have in mind, Mr Bentley?'

The waiter arrived with their drinks before he could answer. He waited until the man had departed, curving long, lean fingers about his glass as he looked across at her. 'To start from the beginning, I'm blessed with a mother who can't grasp the fact that marriage isn't the be all and end all of existence. After enduring her matchmaking gambits for years, I finally struck on the idea of telling her I'd taken the plunge at last on my own initiative. That was three months ago. Now she's been taken ill and wants to see me and meet my wife. Under the circumstances, I can't very well tell her I was lying, hence the need for someone to act the part.'

'Just a minute.' Kim's mind was whirling. 'If the wedding was supposed to be three months ago, how come she hasn't wanted to meet your wife before this?'

'She has,' he said. 'I've managed to put her off by claiming pressure of work.'

'But there had to come a time, surely, when the pretence would have come out anyway?'

'Not necessarily. Plenty of marriages fall apart at the seams during the first few months. Eventually I'd have told her we'd split up, and used the failure as a good reason not to try it again for some time. Like yours, my father died some years ago. Mother married a Canadian and prefers life over there, so there was little danger of her turning up out of the blue.' He paused, assessing her reaction with a faint smile. 'I think that about covers it.'

'Hardly.' Kim drew in a deep breath, still unable to credit that he might be serious. 'It's the most ridiculous thing I ever heard in my life! Even if I agreed, how could you possibly hope to get away with it?'

'That,' he said, 'would depend on how much conviction you put into the role. 'As to agreeing . . .?' He let the question stand for a meaningful second or two. 'You know the alternative.'

'I'm a total stranger to you,' she protested. 'Surely there must be someone else who would help you out?'

'Not without a more permanent contract,' on a cynical note. 'As I said before, I'm not interested in marriage at this stage.'

'Perhaps you should be,' she flashed, trying to find a chink in the armour-plating. 'While the opportunity is still there!' Seeing the sudden mockery in the grey eyes, she wished she had kept her mouth shut. For a man of Ryan Bentley's ilk, opportunity would never be far away. The proposition he had put to her was beyond all reason. There was no way she was going to agree to doing it. Let him do his worst!

And, without jobs, how were she and Tony supposed to live? asked the voice of reason. The man facing her would keep his word, of that she was sure. If she refused him now *she* faced a future devoid of everything worthwhile. Wasn't it worth every effort on her part to stop that happening?

'How long would it be for?' she heard herself asking, without having come to any conscious decision.

'A week at the most,' he said. 'We'd be back for Christmas.'

'But if your mother is ill, you can hardly leave so soon, surely?'

'I doubt she's at death's door,' came the dry retort. 'In fact, I'd go so far as to say she might very well make a miraculous recovery once she gets her way.'

Kim frowned. 'If you know she's only pretending, why bother at all?'

'There's always the chance that this time it's genuine,' he admitted. 'In any case, once she's seen you she'll be reconciled to it.'

Her frown deepened. 'I don't understand. I thought she was the one who wanted you married?'

Firm lips twisted. 'Preferably to someone she already had picked out for me. This way, I can go over there without having to run the gauntlet of persuasion again.'

She searched the lean features, still looking for a way out. 'Couldn't you simply say your wife was unable to make it?'

'That was the plan up to an hour or so ago.' The mockery was there again. 'Never look a gift horse in the mouth.'

'You realise,' she said with deliberation, 'that you become an accessory after the fact as well as a blackmailer?'

There was a sudden dangerous glint in his eyes. 'I can live with it. Of course, any further attempt on your brother's part to divert company funds would be another matter. I'm only willing to let this one go.'

'I can guarantee he won't be doing it again,' she said tautly. 'And I'm not going to thank you for it!'

'Gratitude I can live without.' He sounded totally unmoved. 'Do you want to look at the menu, or shall I order for us both?'

Right at this moment, Kim didn't think herself capable of looking at anything with clear vision. 'Please do,' she agreed stiffly.

He summoned the hovering waiter with a flick of a finger, displaying a wafer-thin gold watch beneath one crisp white cuff. His hands were well kept, but by no means effeminate, Kim noted. There was a look of sinewy strength about them.

A tremor ran down her spine, tensing the muscles in the pit of her stomach. Simple chemistry, she told herself hastily, and not to be confused with emotional response. She was beyond feeling anything but contempt for a man who would deceive his own mother this way—to say nothing of what he was forcing her to do. Serve him right if she dropped him right in it, given half a chance.

## CHAPTER TWO

RYAN ordered the sorrel and cucumber soup followed by turbot *en brioche* for them both. Kim found the first delicious, although she had thought herself beyond enjoying anything in the way of food under present circumstances. Wine was served, providing some measure of comfort in its heady effect.

He waited until the soup was finished and the plates removed before making any attempt to return to the reason she was here at all.

'For the record,' he said purposefully, 'my wife is aged twenty-six and her name is Cassandra—Cass for short.' He cast an appraising glance at Kim's oatmeal tweed suit. 'You're going to need to look the part as well as act it. We'd better do some shopping in the morning.'

'I think I might have other items in my present wardrobe that would pass muster,' she said stiffly.

'Including furs? It's going to be freezing cold in Montreal this time of year.'

'No,' she admitted without regret. 'But isn't that going to prove an expensive investment just for a few days?'

'We'll take it on loan,' he returned imperturbably. 'The rest I'll leave to your discretion. I'm sure your taste is impeccable.'

'Thanks.' Her tone was dry. 'Anything else?'

'Rings,' he said. 'Wedding *and* engagement. It's going to be a busy morning!'

She looked at him for an irresolute moment, hardly yet believing he really intended to go through with this charade. 'Wouldn't it be simpler just to admit the truth?' she asked desperately.

Grey eyes returned her gaze without a flicker. 'Simpler, perhaps, but not a course I intend taking.'

'Because you can't bear to be caught out?'

'My reasons are immaterial.' This time there was no mistaking the intolerant edge to his voice. 'We'll be flying out Thursday morning.'

'That's barely thirty-six hours!' she protested. 'And what am I supposed to tell my brother?'

'Anything you like, barring where and why you'll be going. You surely don't have to answer to him for your every move, do you?'

'That's hardly the point,' she said, but knew it was hopeless belabouring it further. Tony was the least of her problems right now.

She ate little of the meal when it came, excellent though it was. Ryan Bentley kept up a desultory conversation to which she responded in monosyllables. Any physical attraction she might have felt towards him initially had long since flown. The man was without compunction when it came to his own interests.

They were ready to go by nine-thirty. Ryan had a taxi called to the door of the restaurant, instructing the driver to take them to the address Kim gave him. Despite her protests, he insisted on accompanying her to the main door of the flats on arrival.

'I'll pick you up here at ten o'clock,' he said. 'Don't keep me waiting.'

'As if I'd dare,' she returned tartly, conscious of his closeness at her back as she fumbled for her key. 'You have me over a barrel, Mr Bentley, and you know it!'

The chuckle came low and amused. 'Not exactly the turn of phrase I'd have chosen myself, but I appreciate the sentiment.' He put a hand on her shoulder and drew her round to face him, a glint in his eyes as he viewed her wary expression. 'About time we sealed the bargain, don't you think?'

Kim stiffened as he dropped his head to find her mouth, quelling the urge to struggle. His lips were firm and compelling, arousing an involuntary response. She felt her own lips soften and part, felt her body move into closer contact. It took every ounce of will-power she possessed to break the spell and push him roughly away.

'That isn't part of the bargain!' she snapped.

'To a certain extent, it has to be,' came the unmoved response. 'I don't want you stiffening up every time I happen to touch you. We'll be expected to act like any other couple barely three months married— in public, at least. In private, we can revert to our normal selves, of course.'

'What a relief!' She made no effort to keep the scorn from her voice. 'Goodnight, Mr Bentley.'

'You'd better get used to calling me Ryan, Cass,' he said meaningfully. 'Or darling, if it comes any easier.'

She made no reply to that sally. Cassandra. Trust him to come up with some outlandish name! Answering even to the diminutive was going to take some doing.

She heard the taxi draw away again as she was mounting the stairs to the second-floor flat. The imprint of his lips still lingered on hers. She touched the soft flesh with the tip of her tongue, aware of a tremor deep down in the very pit of her stomach. Just a kiss, yet it had left an impression all too rarely experienced before. Physical attraction took little note of the finer emotions, it seemed. One could hate and despise a person and still feel oneself drawn. Nothing about this coming trip was going to be easy, she acknowledged numbly.

Fair-haired, and possessed of looks which usually gained him most of what he wanted, Tony met her at the door. For once his normal insouciance was missing. The blue eyes so like her own were darkened with worry.

'What on earth happened?' he demanded. 'I've been sitting here biting my nails for hours!'

From somewhere, Kim found a reassuring smile. 'It's all taken care of. So far as Unitec are concerned, there was never anything missing.'

'Thank God!' He sounded more jubilant than relieved. 'You're a gem, Kim. A real gem!' He followed her into the small sitting-room, pausing by the door to add plaintively, 'All the same, you took your time getting back.'

'I ran into an old friend,' she said without looking his way. 'I couldn't just walk away.' She drew in a shallow breath. 'As a matter of fact, I've been invited to visit her in Devon. That's where she and her husband are living now.' She was improvising as she went. 'We were at school together.'

'Oh, yes?' Tony's interest was already fading. 'I don't suppose you're thinking of going.'

'I thought I might while I had the chance.' Kim forced herself to turn her head. 'You could manage on your own for a few days, couldn't you?'

'Oh, sure!' His eyes had brightened again. 'Good idea, in fact. It's going to be the last chance of a break you're likely to get for months. When were you thinking of?'

Having the flat to himself would be a real bonus, Kim thought drily, too well aware of the way his mind was working. He would have moved out ages ago if he'd been able to afford a place of his own. As it was, his share of the rent was rarely forthcoming.

'Thursday,' she said. 'A bit short notice, I know, but with Christmas less than two weeks away it's a case of fitting it in.'

'You don't have to worry about me over the holiday,' he returned magnanimously. 'I've plans of my own. Stay as long as you like.'

'Thanks, but a week should be long enough.' Kim was already moving in the direction of her bedroom. 'I'll get changed and see about supper. I don't suppose you ate yet?'

'Just a sandwich,' came the anticipated reply. 'How about you?'

'I had dinner with ... Cassandra.'

Tony laughed. 'Sounds like a character out of a romantic novel!'

Close, she thought sardonically. She closed the door behind her, standing for a brief moment collecting herself before crossing to the wardrobe to extract a housecoat. Taking off the tweed suit, she hung it carefully away, then stripped off her sweater. The dressing-table mirror opposite revealed a trim figure slenderly curved in the brief lacy undergarments. Cut to turn under at the ends on a level with her chin, her hair lay smooth and glossy. Blue-eyed blondes were ten a penny. Why couldn't Ryan Bentley have found himself some other victim?

Because no one else was in a position to be forced, came the all-too-ready answer. She had landed herself in this predicament; it was up to her to carry it through. Only Tony could expect no further help from her in future. From now on, he handled his own mistakes.

It was a long night, and not a restful one. Morning brought no relief from her endlessly circling thoughts. With Tony out of the way, she finished her few chores, then went reluctantly to change for the coming ordeal. There was always the slight possibility that Ryan Bentley would have changed his mind after sleeping on the idea, but she somehow doubted it. He wasn't the type to have second thoughts on any score unless given good sound reason, and she could come up with nothing which might conceivably come under that heading.

She chose a classic grey wool dress and matching coat as the least likely to offend his taste, adding a single strand of pearls and ear-studs and settling for plain black leather accessories. He was already waiting by the taxi when she got outside. He watched her coming with an unreadable expression on his face.

'Playing safe?' he asked with perception when they were seated and the cab was moving off. 'That outfit makes you look ten years older.'

'I *feel* ten years older since last night,' she said shortly. 'No doubt *you* slept the sleep of the just?'

'I slept,' he agreed. 'What did you tell your brother?'

'He thinks I'm going to be visiting a friend in Devon. And no, he doesn't have an address, if that's what you were going to ask.'

'I wasn't,' Ryan denied calmly. 'Your arrangements are your own affair. All I'm interested in is a convincing act.'

'Supposing I turned out to be the world's worst actress?' Kim suggested, with a faint hope that died almost before it formed as she saw the strong mouth twist.

'Women are born actresses. All it takes is incentive. You'll play the part all right. Let me down . . .'

He left it there, but his meaning was unmistakable. It still wouldn't be too late to bring charges. Her and Tony's word was hardly likely to stand up against his if it came to the point. That he was capable, she didn't doubt for a second. Crossed, a man like Ryan Bentley would be without mercy.

Their first port of call proved to be a small, back-street furrier's Kim hadn't even known existed. Ryan had a few private words with the proprietor who, to judge from his smile, seemed perfectly agreeable to whatever arrangement had been suggested. The coats brought out for her to try on took her breath. Fine feathers, she thought, viewing her reflection through the long mirror in a full-length silver fox and matching hat. Glimpsed under this outfit, even the grey dress took on new life.

'That's the one,' said Ryan decisively, echoing her own opinion. 'Keep it on. Your coat can be boxed instead.'

Making her a fit companion to be seen with, at least, she thought with irony. Aloud she said, 'Supposing we run across someone who knows me while I'm wearing it?'

His mouth acquired a cynical line. 'They're going to think you struck lucky.'

If there was any luck entailed in this situation, it had to be all bad, Kim reflected. Explaining the coat away to anyone who did happen to spot her would not be easy. She just had to hope that it wouldn't be necessary.

The rings came next. They went to Cartier, where they were shown into a back office and given comfortable chairs while various trays were fetched from the safe. Lost in the glitter of diamonds, Kim could only murmur agreement when Ryan himself opted for a twisted half-hoop which sat on her finger as if made for it.

Asked to produce wedding-rings in addition, the jeweller expressed no visible surprise. Perhaps he was accustomed to having the whole thing done at one sitting, mused Kim with a cynicism of her own. No spreading the cost in these exalted spheres. Money had to be of little object to anyone who chose to buy their wares here.

Ryan declined to choose a ring for himself. He would probably have done the same, she reflected, had the occasion been genuine. Apart from the slender watch, and a plain gold signet ring on one little finger, he wore no jewellery that she could see. Not the type to sport medallions or chains anyway. Too essentially masculine. She only wished she could stop herself from reacting to that very masculinity.

'I'm going to trust you to pack suitable indoor clothing,' he said when they were in yet another taxi and moving in the direction of Piccadilly. 'I have a lot to do this afternoon.'

'Thanks,' she said drily. 'I'll try to live up to the image.'

'You'd better,' he growled. He paused, added curtly, 'Look, let's agree to forget the smart retorts and act like a normal couple, shall we?'

'Depends what you call normal,' she came back. 'Some married couples I've seen seem to spend their whole time bickering.'

'Only because the husband isn't man enough to wear the trousers. Give a woman too much rope and she loses all sense of proportion.'

'From which I gather any woman you eventually marry will have to toe the line or suffer the consequences?'

The mockery seemed to amuse rather than annoy him. 'That's right. I've heard there's a Scottish law, never rescinded, which allows a man to put his wife across his knee if she misbehaves.'

'You're not Scottish,' she pointed out, refusing to rise to the taunt.

'That doesn't stop me from following the example set. My stepfather would probably be the first to applaud such tactics. He's French-Canadian, and very much into masculine superiority.' The smile was faint.

'Not that it gets him very far with my mother. She has a will like a mule.'

'Like mother, like son,' Kim responded caustically. 'I'm surprised you allowed yourself to be pushed this far in the first place.'

'One swallow doth not a summer make,' he remarked with meaningful inflexion. 'To get back to the original question, do you intend keeping this up?'

Blue eyes met grey, neither pair giving way. 'That depends,' she said, 'on the provocation. You might have forced me into this position, Ryan, *darling*, but you need me to carry the thing through.'

There was a steely glint in the grey. 'If that's a threat,' he said on a silky note, 'it's a particularly foolish one.'

Kim was inclined to agree, but nothing would have persuaded her to back down at that moment. 'Call it an observation,' she rejoined, and wondered at her own self-command. Dressed to kill, with a mind to match, she thought with a flash of humour. In this coat she felt equal to anything—or anyone.

Conversation, if it could be called that, lapsed for the rest of the journey. Ryan looked meditative, as if just beginning to realise what he might have taken on—or so she hoped. It would do him good to be taken down a peg or two from that high and mighty attitude of his. Superior sex, indeed! For the first time she was starting to appreciate her position in this affair. Once they were over there, with the deception up and running, so to speak, the ball would be equally in her court.

She gained a further boost to her esteem from the solicitous attention paid by the doorman at the Ritz

when they arrived. Once inside, she made her way to
the ladies' cloakroom to leave both her coat and the
box containing her own garment in the care of the
attendant. Shorn of the former, she felt her confidence slipping a little, and made a determined effort
to retain it. The dress she was wearing had class
enough to hold its own in any company—Ryan's in-
cluded. From now on, she played the part all the way
through.

Pre-lunch drinks were served in the lounge. Kim
stuck stubbornly to her usual dry sherry, unable to
stop her glance from drifting to a nearby group where
a certain well-known star of film and theatre was
holding court. There were several other recognisable
faces in the room too. Who's who in Wonderland?
she thought whimsically, trying to put names to them
all.

A couple just coming up the steps from the lower
level caught her eye. As dark as her companion was
fair, the woman was outstanding in her exotic beauty.
All of five feet nine or ten inches tall, and slender as
a reed in the superbly cut red dress and jacket, she
carried herself like a queen.

She was aware, too, Kim realised, of the interest
she was causing. It was there in the haughty turn of
her glossy head as she surveyed the scene. Her glance
came to rest on their table, her expression undergoing
a subtle alteration. She said something to the man at
her side, then the two of them were coming over, the
full red mouth breaking into a smile scheduled to set
most male hearts beating faster.

'I didn't expect to see you here this morning, Ryan,'
she said smoothly.

'I didn't expect to be here,' he returned, equally smoothly. 'Are you lunching?'

'Of course!'

'Then perhaps you'd care to join us for a drink first?'

The smile was too fixed, Kim thought, as the other murmured assent. Then she was finding a smile herself as Ryan performed introductions. Georgina Gregory—the name suited the woman. Fleetingly, Kim wondered if it was real or assumed. The man was called Roger Courtland. Handsome as any film star, he had little to say for himself. Dressing only, Kim found herself concluding.

Ryan's relationship with the beautiful brunette was less easy to define. There was intimacy in the way she looked at him, true, but no discernible answer in the grey eyes. Not that his lack of expression meant lack of involvement, by any means, came the cynical thought. He probably had affairs going all over the place!

He made no attempt to outline her own supposed role in his life, for which she was thankful. Georgina, she learned, was a fashion model at present under contract to one of the top houses. Her whole conversation was centred on her future career prospects, interesting enough to a point, but eye-glazing after several minutes.

There was *no* way, Kim told herself with emphasis, that a man of Ryan Bentley's undoubted intelligence could align himself in any way but the purely physical with a woman so devoid of the former commodity. All the same, she envied that face. Looks like that were the 'open sesame' to a totally different world from the one she inhabited.

Much to her relief, there was no suggestion that they eat together, although she had the feeling that Georgina would not have turned up her nose at any such invitation. They were actually several tables away from each other when they finally went through. With wine in her glass and a warm glow spreading inside, Kim felt emboldened enough to relax the guard she had put on her tongue this past half-hour.

'I suppose,' she said lightly, 'that an empty head imposes little strain on a man after a hard day's work. That in itself must have its attractions.'

'If you're talking about Georgina,' Ryan returned on a similar note, 'it does. With her, I always know exactly where I am.'

'You're actually admitting there are times when you don't?' The mockery was deliberated, the widening of her eyes a goad to the spark already leaping in the ones opposite. 'Oh, Ryan, you do surprise me!'

One tanned hand snaked across the table to cover hers where it lay on the cloth, fingers curving with a feel of tensile strength. 'I've a notion,' he said softly, 'that you and I are going to have to reach more than one kind of understanding before we're through, my sweet. You're too lippy by half!'

'I'm over last night's shock,' she retorted, trying to ignore the sensation created by his touch. 'What you see is what you get. Of course, if you want to call the whole thing off...'

'No way!' The intonation was forceful. 'Having come this far, I've no intention of backing out.'

'It takes a big man to admit a mistake,' Kim rejoined, not about to let the moment pass. 'Why not do yourself a favour?'

'Perhaps because I'm not quite big enough,' he acknowledged grimly. 'Only don't let that fool you into thinking I might turn out to be a soft touch after all. I stand by everything I've said.'

Looking into the hard-boned features, she was fleetingly tempted to put him to the test—but only fleetingly. She couldn't take the risk. Not with her new job hanging in the balance.

The strong mouth pulled into a narrow smile when she failed to come up with any further reply. 'That's better. A little more practice, and you might even find yourself enjoying the role.'

'Not,' she said bitterly, 'in a million years! If you were the last man on earth I still wouldn't choose you as a mate!'

His laugh was low. 'If I were the last man on earth, you'd have to stand in line with the rest!'

There was no answer to that. None, at least, that she could think of off the top of her head. It was doubly infuriating to be left high and dry.

He was still holding her hand down on the table. As if to further her frustration, he lifted it to his lips and pressed a taunting kiss on the back. Kim snatched it away as if stung, twin spots of colour high on her cheekbones. He knew how he affected her; he had to know. It was there in his eyes, in the slant of his lips, in the whole hateful manner he had adopted towards her. Only he needn't think it would make *her* any soft touch either. She knew her worth.

They left at two-fifteen after a meal to which Kim had done full justice regardless of everything. If she had to be part of his charade, she might as well take advantage of the perks, she thought.

The young woman who was talking to Ryan when she came up from the cloakroom was a vastly different proposition from Georgina. Striking rather than beautiful, with hair the colour of old mahogany, she looked capable of holding her own in any company. The two of them were laughing, as if at some shared joke. Already in sight, Kim had no alternative but to join them.

'Kimberly Anderson—Chloe Bryant,' he said easily.

Emerald-green eyes took in every detail both of the grey dress and the coat slung over her arm, reaching, Kim was sure, an immediate and accurate assessment of both items. The smile seemed friendly enough, until one realised it only touched her mouth.

'Must dash,' she said. 'I've an appointment in ten minutes. Nice to have met you.' The glance she turned back to Ryan revealed little. 'You haven't forgotten the Jamiesons' party next week?'

'I hadn't,' he acknowledged, 'but I'm afraid I'm going to be out of the country. I already phoned Susan.'

There was a flash of what could have been disappointment in the other eyes, though the smile remained fixed. 'You'll be back before the holiday, I hope?'

'Should be,' he agreed. 'I'll be in touch.'

'There's no doubt, I hope,' Kim commented softly as the woman departed. 'About getting back, I mean? You said it would only be for a week.'

'So it will.' He took the coat from her, holding it for her to slide her arms into the sleeves. 'Stop worrying.'

Stop worrying! She wanted to laugh. Last week at this time she'd had nothing *to* worry about. Now she had everything. Just let him try to extend the terms of their contract, that was all!

'I'm going to put you in a taxi,' he said. 'I have to go in to the office. I want you ready and waiting by eleven tomorrow. OK?'

The question was purely rhetorical; she didn't have any other choice. Kim inclined her head, not meeting his eyes as he moved round into view again. By this time tomorrow they would be in the air heading west. Not exactly the way she would have chosen to make her first Atlantic crossing, but still something of a milestone in her life. It was the thought of meeting Ryan's mother—of deceiving a sick woman—that bothered her the most. If it were only possible to turn back the clock on these past few days.

# CHAPTER THREE

GAZING down on the billowing white cloud cover a
thousand feet below, Kim wondered what the weather
was doing at sea-level. Cocooned in the luxury of the
first-class cabin, she felt out of touch with the real
world.

Her departure from the flat this morning had
brought unforeseen problems. She would never forget
the look on her neighbour's face on seeing her wearing
the coat and hat which had spent the night hidden
away in her wardrobe from Tony's eyes. If any
mention was made to her brother, she was going to
have some explaining to do when she got back.
However, that would be then. She had enough to
worry about for the present.

Seated at her side, Ryan looked totally relaxed. He
had turned up wearing a sheepskin coat over casual
trousers and tweedy jacket, the first now removed, of
course, and hung carefully away by the stewardess,
along with her own, in the locker provided. If he had
any worries at all concerning the coming reunion with
his mother, he had shown no sign so far. But then,
he had to be devoid of all conscience to do what he'd
done in the first place, didn't he?

The more she thought about it, the more she re-
gretted not telling him to go to hell while she'd had
the chance. He might even have respected her enough
for it to let her go free.

And pigs might fly! said a cynical little voice at the back of her mind. Her fate had been sealed from the moment he'd hit on the idea of using her.

'There's no turning back now,' he said levelly, as if reading her thoughts. 'We're both of us stuck with the situation.'

'Does that mean you're starting to recognise the possible pitfalls at last?' Kim asked with deliberation, and drew a response in the turn of the dark head towards her.

'There'd better not be any. I'm relying on you to be convincing.'

She met his gaze without flinching. 'Always provided I'm not expected to fawn all over you like some love-struck idiot!'

His lips twitched. 'I'll settle for the occasional besotted glance. My stepfather may have French blood running through his veins, but the Canadian half takes precedence when it comes to emotional display, so *he'll* not be looking for too much outward show from either of us.'

'How very reassuring.' She was silent for a moment or two, marshalling her reserves. 'What about sleeping arrangements?' she made herself ask. 'Shall we be expected to share a room?'

'Naturally. Bathroom, too. Twin beds should provide enough privacy.'

'For you, perhaps,' she retorted. 'Not for me!'

He shrugged. 'Hobson's choice, I'm afraid. Separate rooms went out with the Victorians. What are you afraid of? I already told you I don't have any designs on your body.'

If she were honest with herself, that rejection actually stung, Kim admitted wryly. His kiss the other night had stirred something in her that needed no encouragement, so it should be a relief that he intended no repeat performance. To find herself becoming in any way emotionally involved with a man of Ryan Bentley's ilk was the last thing she'd want.

'I imagine,' she said with a studied coolness, 'it will make quite a change for you to sleep with a woman in the proper sense of the word!'

'There's nothing improper in the other sense,' he returned. 'Not unless you find the whole act unnatural.' His glance dropped from her face to the thrust of her breasts against the thin silk of her dress, his mouth taking on a slant. 'From the way you're reacting right now, I'd say that was unlikely.'

Kim's face burned. She could feel her nipples pressing against the material of her brassière—the warmth spreading from the pit of her stomach. If he could arouse her this far with just a look, how was she going to cope with the intimacy of the coming week? No designs on her body, he'd said, but would that statement stand up to the provocation of knowing how he affected her?

'You read too much into too little,' she retorted stonily. 'What time do we land?'

He accepted the change of subject without demur, though there was no ignoring the mocking light in his eyes. 'Around three-fifteen. It's going to be gone four by the time we clear the airport. Mike is meeting us himself.'

'Mike?'

'My stepfather.' Dark brows lifted. 'Why the surprise? I'm hardly going to "Daddy" a man only twenty years my senior.'

'I was expecting a more French-sounding name, that's all.'

'Is Michael Dubois French-sounding enough for you? Not that he looks Gallic, anyway. He takes after his mother who was pure-bred American. Mike's a self-made man. Started out with nothing and achieved everything.'

Kim said softly, 'I gather you admire him.'

He laughed. 'I'd admire any man able to take on my mother without going under!'

'You make her sound a real battle-axe.'

'No,' he said, 'just a woman who knows exactly what she wants and intends having it. Mostly, we get along very well.'

'Until your aims cross.' Kim hesitated. 'Am I likely to come under fire for upsetting her plans?'

'Maybe.' His tone was lacking in concern. 'One of the reasons you came across as so eminently suitable for the role was your ability to stand up under attack.'

'I'm flattered.' The sarcasm was muted by trepidation for what was to come. 'One of these days, you're going to fall flat on your calculating face, Ryan Bentley. I only hope I'm somewhere around to see it happen!'

'Unlikely,' came the unmoved response, leaving her to guess whether he was referring to the latter desire or the former statement. If the first, he was more than likely right, she acknowledged, quelling the sudden despondency engendered by the thought. Once they got back to England, he would simply follow his original plan of announcing a break-up of the marriage in due course, leaving no reason for them ever to meet again.

They were ten minutes early into Mirabel. Emerging into the arrivals hall, Ryan lifted a hand to wave to someone standing among the crowd of people on the glassed-in balcony above, but Kim was unable to pick out which of those waving back was the recipient. Baggage claim was the customary shambles, but they had no trouble getting through Customs.

The man who stepped forward to greet them as they came out through the double doors was the total antithesis of her mental image. As tall as Ryan himself, he had the build of an all-American football player, with shoulders that would need no padding. A thick sweep of silvered fair hair topped craggy, good-natured features.

'Good to see you!' he exclaimed, shaking his stepson's hand with enthusiasm. 'You too, Cass,' he added, and treated Kim to an embrace that left her breathless. 'Guessed you'd have to be a looker. No son of Lydia's would settle for less than the best!'

'Nice of you to say so, Mr Dubois,' she murmured a little dazedly, not sure whether she should make that *Monsieur*.

'Make it Mike,' he invited, removing the problem. 'Let's get on the way. We can talk in the car.'

Grey eyes briefly met blue as they all three moved in the direction of the outer doors, the former revealing amusement. Nothing he had said about the Canadian could have prepared her for the reality, Kim acknowledged. Michael Dubois was possessed of a quality one had to meet to appreciate.

Warned though she had been of the winter temperatures normally to be found at these latitudes, she was unprepared for the sheer, breath-robbing iciness of the air outside the heated building. Gasping, she clutched the fur closer about her throat, only too grateful to pile into the rear seat of the Lincoln Continental Mike had left parked with blithe unconcern for the airport rules.

'Never got towed away yet,' he said in answer to Ryan's comment. 'First time it happens, I guess I might think again. OK in the back there?'

'Fine,' Kim assured him, already warming up again in the flow of hot air through the vehicle's air-conditioning system. 'I just wasn't ready for that degree of cold.'

'Gets a whole lot colder than this when you take in wind-chill,' he observed. 'You'll soon adjust once your circulation gets pepped up. A lot healthier climate than your London pea-soupers, I can tell you.'

'We haven't had those in years,' put in his stepson. 'Shows how long it is since you were over.' There was a pause, a change of tone. 'How's Mother?'

'Hanging in.' The craggy features hadn't altered, but the note in his voice was expressive of a certain censure. 'Better for knowing you were on your way. She's looking forward to meeting you at last, Cass. Not that she's going to give you an easy time of it, considering she missed the wedding.'

'We neither of us wanted any fuss making,' said Ryan smoothly. 'I already explained all that.'

'You'll be facing the music yourself,' the older man warned him. 'She's got a few words saved up that need airing.'

'After which all will be well, I imagine,' came the ironic reply.

There was a lengthy pause before Mike answered. When he did it was without inflexion. 'She wouldn't thank me for telling you, but I guess you've a right to know. Her heart's going. Another attack like the one she just had, and it could be the last.'

Listening from the back, Kim saw Ryan's head jerk as if from a blow. She had a sudden urge to put a hand on his shoulder in comfort—except that any such move would probably be misconstrued. He'd given little impression of deep feeling where his mother was concerned, anyway, from the way he'd spoken of her. Why should he have need of comfort? They were here for the simple reason that his hand had been forced.

'She's seen a specialist?' he asked after a moment.

'Two,' Mike confirmed. 'They both gave the same verdict. She mustn't be put under any undue stress. Not that it's made the least bit of difference to her— on the surface, at any rate. I'd as soon you didn't let on that you know, either. The last thing she'd want is sympathy.'

Which put paid to any plans she might have had for making Ryan sweat, acknowledged Kim wryly. If Ryan had a single decent atom left in him, he would confess the whole thing.

Hardly advisable, though, under the circumstances, was it? came the rider. Any such confession now could well induce the very state to be avoided at all costs. They were stuck with the lie, and must make the best of it. Perhaps after this he would give a little more thought to his actions.

Once away from the airport environs, they were in a glistening white world. Apart from a couple of skiing holidays in the Alps, Kim had never seen so much snow, although the roads were clear. The Dubois lived some distance out of Montreal itself. Even using the autoroutes, it took over an hour to drive there, with little to see in the dark.

Leaving the freeway at last, they entered a wooded area where lit buildings were few and far between. Rural in the extreme, Kim thought, listening to the sound of hard-packed snow scrunching beneath the wheels. Then they were turning into an unfenced driveway and heading for a large house set well back and lit like a Christmas tree.

'Home,' announced Mike on a note of quiet satisfaction.

Pressing a key-pad to open electronically controlled doors, he drove the car straight in to a garage big enough to hold three similar-sized vehicles. The only other one there at present was a pale blue Cadillac. While a good deal lower than the heated interior of the car, the temperature was still considerably higher than that outside, much to Kim's relief. Not even the silver fox could provide long-term protection against such cold.

A door in the side wall gave access to the house itself. Beyond was a wide hallway lit by a crystal chandelier and carpeted in a silver-grey echoed in the paler tint of the walls. Several fine paintings brought both colour and character to the room.

The woman who appeared in one of the archways opening off was statuesque in appearance, her hair blue-rinsed and superbly coiffured. A handsome woman, Kim conceded, her relationship with Ryan evidenced both in the strength of feature and the penetrating sharpness of the grey eyes.

'So you're the one who finally managed to pin this son of mine down,' she commented without preamble. 'Not quite what I imagined.'

'What *did* you imagine?' asked Kim on a light note, and drew the faintest of smiles.

'Some brassy blonde with an eye open to the main chance comes close enough.'

Her son laughed, moving forward to press a swift kiss to her cheek. 'You don't give me much credit for taste. Cass is more than just a pretty face, she's a career girl to boot.' He held out a hand, the smile on his lips as easy and natural as if nothing at all were untoward about the moment. 'Come and say a proper hello to your mother-in-law, darling.'

Kim obeyed the injunction because she had no alternative, steeling herself to meet the eyes she was certain could see right through her. On impulse, she leaned forward and kissed the same cheek Ryan had kissed. 'I'm happy to be here,' she murmured.

It was difficult to tell whether the gesture had pleased the older woman or not. If anything, she seemed taken aback.

'Better late than never, I suppose,' she conceded grudgingly. 'You'll want to freshen up before supper. I put you in the guest suite, Ryan. You know where it is.'

'I'll bring one up,' offered Mike as the younger man moved back to where he had left the two suitcases.

'No problem,' Ryan assured him, hefting one in each hand. 'I'm lucky in having a wife who believes in travelling light.' His glance in Kim's direction held just the right amount of affectionate mockery. 'Just one of her good points.'

'I have others you didn't even discover yet,' she responded, matching his tone. 'Lead on, I'll follow.'

She was aware of Lydia Dubois's gaze on her back as she mounted the thickly carpeted staircase in Ryan's wake, and was thankful to turn right at the top down a wide corridor, instead of left along the open gallery.

The room they were to share lay at the rear of the house. Beautifully furnished and decorated, it invited more than a cursory inspection, but Kim had eyes only for the king-sized bed occupying a central position against the far wall.

'You said twin beds!' she accused, refusing to move further than the doorway. 'There's no way I'm going to share *that* with you!'

Ryan dropped both cases to the floor and came back to seize her by the wrist, drawing her forcibly inside the room and closing the door. 'Before you give the whole game away,' he said tautly, 'I wasn't aware there were any double beds in the place! It's unfortunate, but we'll simply have to manage.'

'No!' Her face was pale and set, eyes like deep blue sapphires in their angry sparkle. 'You'll have to ask for another room!'

Her anger was reflected in the sudden steely glint. 'And what reason am I supposed to give?'

'I don't know. Anything you like!' She was too incensed to care how difficult he might find it to meet that demand. 'The only thing I do know is that I'm *not* sleeping in the same bed with you!'

Jaw jutting, he said tensely, 'You don't have any choice. Neither do I. You heard what Mike said in the car. No upset of any kind. How do you think she'd react to the news that my wife can't even bear to occupy the same bed?'

'With relief, I should think, if what you said about her preferring to pick a wife for you herself was true.' The furnace-fed heat of the house was getting to her, still wrapped as she was in the thick fur. 'Your plans for an incompatibility separation in the not-too-distant future aren't going to look too convincing unless you lay some groundwork down to start with, are they? Separate beds would at least suggest a basis.'

'You'd better take the coat off,' he observed, ignoring the last. 'Before you pass out.'

He had already shed his own outer wear downstairs. Too stifled to argue, she tore the hat from her head and tossed it across the room, dropping the coat on the floor where she stood. 'So much for the trappings,' she stated contemptuously. 'You might have managed to blackmail me this far, but you're in no position to take it any further without my willing co-operation.'

'Is that a fact?' His voice was silky soft, and dangerous with it. 'Then we'd better give some thought to making you willing.'

He reached for her again before she had time to side-step. Not, she was bound to admit, that there was anywhere she could have run to to escape him. She pummelled at him with her free fist as he carried her across to the bed, but it made little impression.

The drop on to the mattress robbed her of her breath for a moment. She felt his weight pinning her

down, felt the whole muscular length of him covering
her body. His strength was prodigious; there was no
fighting the hand holding her head steady as he found
her mouth.

Ruthless though the pressure was, she found herself
responding to it, lips softening, melting, opening to
let him in. Rational thought retreated to a distance at
which it had no bearing on what was happening to
her. There was a pounding in her ears, a pulsating
heat spreading through her whole body. The thrust
of his hand inside the opened front of her dress
brought no sense of rejection. She wanted his touch
at her breast, she realised; had wanted it since that
first time he had kissed her. He lowered his head to
take her hardened nipple between his lips, using
tongue and teeth until she wanted to scream at the
sheer agony he was inflicting on the tender flesh. Yet
at the same time she was holding him there, fingers
curling into the thick dark hair, limbs shifting beneath him in totally involuntary invitation.

Dropping a knee between her thighs, he pressured
them open, fitting himself to her in a manner that
brought the blood rushing to her head. He was
aroused himself; that much she couldn't doubt. If he
kept this up she wouldn't be able to say no—wouldn't
be able to even want to say no. All she wanted was
release from the desperate need filling every corner
of her mind and body. Release, and fulfilment of a
kind only dreamed of.

She bit back the quivering plea by sheer effort of
will when he lifted himself abruptly away from her.
Breathing harder, but still well in control, he said
grimly, 'We'll save the rest for another time, shall we?'

'There won't be another time,' she whispered through the sawdust in her throat. 'I loathe you, Ryan! More than I ever loathed anyone!'

His smile was cruel. 'It doesn't stop you wanting me, though. I could have taken you without a solitary protest on your part just now, and we both of us know it. Be a good girl, and I may even oblige. Keep on threatening me, and frustration isn't the only thing you'll be suffering.'

She lay still as he got to his feet. The fact that he'd spoken the truth didn't help. What was happening to her, that she could sink so far? Did sexual satisfaction mean so much that she could actually contemplate seeking it through a man like Ryan Bentley? Since the moment she'd set eyes on him, he had exercised a fatal fascination over her. Only not any more. From this moment on she would fight it with her last breath!

'Hadn't you better think about tidying yourself up?' he asked when she failed to move. 'We're expected downstairs for supper, in case you'd forgotten.' He cast her a glance as she pushed herself reluctantly upright, his smile derisive. 'Not quite so much to say for yourself now, I see.'

'Only because the words don't exist that would be adequate for the way I feel,' she responded tightly. 'You're despicable!'

'Disreputable at times, I'll grant you,' he returned, already moving away. 'We're in this together, we'll see it through together.'

'And afterwards?' She flung the words at his departing back. 'We spend the next week convincing your mother that everything in the garden is lovely, and then what?'

He made no answer to that. Chiefly because, Kim concluded, he didn't have an answer. She swung her feet to the floor as he disappeared into what she assumed was the en-suite bathroom, aware of a certain shakiness in her limbs. The front of her dress was still opened to the waist, her brief lacy brassière ripped at the centre seam by that ruthless hand. She would have to change, which meant waiting for Ryan to emerge from the bathroom, because she certainly wasn't doing it in here!

Lifting her own suitcase on to the bed, she opened it up to extract the necessary items. She might as well take a quick shower while she was about it. Supper was hardly going to be waiting on the table for them.

Ryan had apparently had the same idea; she could hear water running. Unless he put on the same clothes he had taken off, which seemed unlikely, he would be coming out of there stark naked when he finished. No doubt that would worry him not at all—he was probably quite accustomed to displaying his masculine charms—but her equanimity was far from tried and tested.

She was in at the deep end in more ways than the one, she acknowledged ruefully. The whole situation was fraught with danger.

# CHAPTER FOUR

RYAN had a towel slung about his hips when he eventually emerged. Kim averted her eyes from direct confrontation, but nothing could shut out the mental image of smooth-muscled shoulders and arms, of the broad, deep chest lightly coated in black hair, of a stomach as flat and taut as a board, and hard-hewn thighs.

It might have helped a little if he'd at least had bony knees, she thought ironically. As a physical specimen, he was superbly equipped. A pity his spiritual qualities failed to measure up.

'It's all yours,' he said. 'Just remember we don't have all evening.'

'Unlike the women you're apparently accustomed to, I'm not in the habit of spending hours in the bathroom,' she retorted tartly. 'I'll be ready in ten minutes.'

She made it in nine and a half. Make-up refreshed, hair brushed into shining order, and wearing a dress in fine, off-white wool, she returned to the bedroom to find Ryan, in trousers and silky, roll-necked sweater, just about to slide his feet into a pair of casual shoes.

'Glad to see you're a woman of your word,' he commented drily. 'Ready to bite the bullet again?'

'As I'll ever be,' she acknowledged, smothering her less agreeable inclinations. 'Is there anything in Cass's background that you haven't told me about, by any chance?' she tagged on with intent. 'I'd hate to slip up on the story.'

His smile was thin. 'Nothing you can't make up as you go along. Shouldn't be too much of a problem to someone with your turn of phrase.' He stood up from the chair, tall, dark and intractable. 'Let's get it over with.'

The Dubois were waiting for them in the magazine-cover sitting-room. Designer-decorated and furnished, Lydia admitted readily enough in answer to Kim's admiring comment. She had more to do in life than spend days and weeks agonising over colour schemes and fabric samples.

'So what exactly is this career of yours?' she asked over supper in the lime and apricot dining-room. 'Ryan didn't mention it before.'

'I'm in computing,' Kim acknowledged, thinking it best to stick as closely as possible to the truth. 'A systems programmer at present, with aspirations towards becoming an analyst in the not-too-distant future.'

'Sounds impressive,' said Mike. 'Time-consuming too, I'd guess, though.'

'No more than any other worthwhile job.'

'What he means,' put in Lydia, 'is that a career is going to leave you little time for family commitments. Children are a full-time job in themselves.'

'We only just got married,' protested her son on a light note. 'Give it a chance!'

'You're thirty-five now,' she returned equably. 'Another few years, and you'll be past enjoying the patter of little feet. You *do* want children, I take it?' The last to Kim herself.

Startled, she said, 'Well, yes. I . . . just don't think there's any great rush, that's all.'

Mike laughed. 'You sound like my daughter. Time for everything, that's her maxim!'

Kim turned to him, grateful for any change of subject. 'I didn't realise you had a daughter.'

'Ryan didn't tell you?' The glance he directed at his stepson was quizzical. 'I guess you've both been too busy to get round to sharing reminiscences. Eloise runs a boutique downtown. She's up in Ottawa right now visiting with friends. She'll be back tomorrow.'

'Unless she decides to stay on a while longer.' Lydia sounded oddly abrupt. 'Is everyone ready for dessert?'

There was some undercurrent here, Kim reflected, murmuring assent. Something involving both Ryan and Eloise, if she read the signs correctly. There was little to be gleaned from his expression, but then there rarely was unless he intended to impart. If he played poker he would win every hand!

Apart from one or two minor hiccups, the rest of the evening passed pleasantly enough. Without prior warning, Lydia's condition would have remained a secret. There was certainly nothing in her attitude to suggest any preoccupation with the sentence passed on her, nor any physical sign of deteriorating health.

'You must be tired after the journey,' she said to Kim around ten o'clock, seeing her stifle a yawn. 'Staying up until three in the morning seems ridiculous, but it's the only way to get over the time change. Otherwise, you'd find yourself wakening up in the early hours.'

'You go on up,' invited Ryan easily. 'I'll be along myself in a few minutes.'

Don't rush, Kim wanted to tell him. Take all the time you like! Aloud, she said smoothly, 'I'll say goodnight, then. And thank you once again, Mrs Dubois, for a lovely meal.'

'If you can't manage Mother you'd better call me Lydia,' came the dry response. 'Goodnight, Cassandra.'

That was one name she was never going to become accustomed to, Kim told herself as she climbed the stairs. Why couldn't Ryan have picked something short and simple?

Because he relished complication, came the answer. If there were two paths to climb, he would no doubt always choose the one which presented the greatest challenge to ingenuity.

The thought of the night to come in his company brought a feeling close to panic. Should he make any further move towards her, she doubted her ability to turn away. Which made her little better than he was himself when it came right down to it. And *that* thought didn't help at all.

Of the two nightdresses she had packed, neither provided what she regarded as adequate cover against close encounter. Short of putting a couple of pillows down the centre of the bed, there was nothing to stop them rolling together by accident while asleep. Ryan had made no attempt to hide his arousal earlier, which hardly reassured her. His moral fibre had already shown itself to be sadly lacking.

She was in bed with the covers drawn up to her chin when he did come up. He made no comment, but simply began undressing. Lying there, head turned towards the window, she heard the double thud as his

shoes were dropped to the floor, followed by the unmistakable rasp of a zip. She let out pent-up breath
when the bathroom door closed. There were several
more nights to get through after this. Was she going
to spend all of them in dread of what might conceivably happen, or was she going to make it clear
here and now that she would brook no repeat of the
earlier performance?

It seemed bare seconds later when the bathroom
door opened again. Hunching herself up as small as
possible, she waited for him to slide in between the
sheets after he turned off the bedside lamp she had
left burning. His approach around to her side of the
bed brought her heart thudding up into her throat.

'Move over,' he invited.

Fury at the sheer, unmitigated gall of the man jerked
her upright. Eyes blazing blue fire, she almost spat
the words at him.

'Touch me again and I'll scream my head off! And
I shan't care who hears me either!'

He lifted a well-schooled eyebrow as he studied her
flushed face, a sardonic slant to the corners of his
mouth. He was wearing the bottom half of a pair of
black silk pyjamas, his chest muscles clearly defined
by the shaft of moonlight streaking through the
window.

'I always sleep on my right side,' he said. 'As I take
it you'd rather I had my back to you, that means I
sleep this side of the bed.'

'Supposing I always sleep on my right side too?'
Kim demanded, refusing to be hoodwinked by the glib
reply.

'Then you'll have to face my back. Safe enough for you?' He made a sudden impatient gesture. 'Look, I'm too tired to even think about starting anything, so for God's sake let's stop playing games, shall we? Either move over, or be put. It's up to you.'

Kim moved without another word to the far edge of the bed, and turned her back on him. She was trembling all over. Damn him! she thought fiercely. He had done that deliberately.

The mattress made little appreciable movement as he lay down. The space between them could have held another body without overcrowding. Kim lay gazing into the darkness until the deepening of his breathing told her he was asleep. Only then did she ease her position, but it was a long time before she slept herself.

White light filled the room when she opened her eyes again. She had been dreaming about a camping holiday she had once been on—she could still feel the snug warmth of the sleeping bag wrapped close about her. A tent pole had fallen across her waist, she thought mistily, then came suddenly and jerkily wide awake in realisation of what the warm weight really was.

Ryan stirred at her back, his hand sliding up to find her breast in a movement so natural that it took her breath away for a moment. They were fitted together like two peas in a pod, his knees bent up under hers, his chest up against her shoulder-blades, his breath tickling her nape where her hair had parted. In that brief moment she was aware with every fibre of the hard strength in that superbly fit body—aware too of the reaction in her own.

'Take your hands off me!' she bit out, and tried to free herself from the all-enveloping embrace. Failing, she dug her nails into the back of the hand still holding her breast, eliciting a muttered curse and a sudden sharp movement that brought her round flat on to her back to look straight into glinting grey eyes.

'Like to play rough, eh?' he growled.

Kim went rigid as he found her mouth. He had a leg thrown across hers at knee-level, effectively pinning her down. The hand which had covered her breast was now at her throat, not hurting her, but not allowing her any choice either. She was forced to suffer the kiss—if suffer was the right word. Even at this hour and in these circumstances, she could feel the stirring of response.

'Relax,' he murmured, lifting his head at last. 'You want it as much as I do.'

'No!' She forced the word between gritted teeth. 'You promised me there wouldn't be any of this. Don't you have *any* conscience?'

His laugh came low. 'Right now it's fighting a losing battle with rather more pressing interests. You don't leave a man much option.'

She caught her lower lip between her teeth as his hand began a slow exploration of her body. His touch was so infinitely gentle, little more than a brushing of his fingertips as he followed the slender line of her leg up over hip and waist to finally reach her breast again. She was past stopping him from drawing down the narrow strap of her nightdress to expose the firm curve, even if he'd been prepared to allow it; past caring about anything but the look in his eyes as he studied her; the mingling of fear and excitement bubbling up inside her; the uncontrollable tremors radiating out to encompass every part of her body. It was going to happen, and she was going to let it. Because she couldn't stop it; because she didn't even want to stop it.

He drew down the other strap to bare her fully to his gaze. Instinctively, she arched her back to lift the firm curves into greater prominence, thrilling to the sudden flare of passion in his eyes. His lips scorched her taut nipples, drawing agonised little moans to her throat. She had never known such exquisite pleasure as this. There was a growing hunger in her for more—for everything.

The knock on the door came like a dash of cold water in the face. Ryan swore under his breath as she stiffened beneath him, then rolled abruptly away from her. There was just time for her to pull up the straps of her nightdress again before the door opened to admit Mrs Dubois carrying a tray.

'I thought breakfast in bed, considering it's your first morning,' she announced. 'Just coffee and toast. You can always have something else when you get down if you feel like it.'

You shouldn't be carrying anything heavy, it was on the tip of Kim's tongue to remark. Just in time, she remembered they weren't supposed to know the true extent of her condition.

'That's very thoughtful of you,' she said instead, making up for Ryan who seemed disinclined to say anything at all. She hoped her smile was less rigid than it felt. 'Thank you.'

The return smile was still a little wintry. 'Eloise rang to say she'd be home some time this afternoon. She's looking forward to meeting you.'

'Oh, good.' Kim could think of no other comment to make. She wished Ryan would say something— anything—instead of lying there with that wooden expression on his face. He wasn't the only one suffering from shock, for heaven's sake! It was only just beginning to dawn on her just how close she had come to giving herself to him without even a token struggle.

His mother deposited the tray on the bedside table nearest to Kim, and left them to it. Only when the door had closed again did he stir, reaching out to run a fingertip down her spine as she leaned to pick up the coffee-pot.

'Where were we?' he queried softly.

Kim got hastily from the bed in order to pour the two cups of coffee. 'Drink it while it's hot,' she said, holding one out to him. 'It smells wonderful!'

'So do you,' he growled. 'Put that down and come on back here. We've some unfinished business to take care of.'

'No.' She tried to keep her tone free of emotion. 'I changed my mind.'

He propped himself on an elbow, eyes narrowed and dangerous. 'Get a kick out of playing that kind of game, do you?'

Still holding the cup, she said stiffly, 'It wasn't a game. You're very... persuasive.'

His smile was brief. 'So let me do some more persuading.'

'No!' This time her voice had an unmistakable shake. 'I'm not here to provide you with extracurricular entertainment. You promised to leave me alone!'

'That was before I realised just how damned difficult it was going to be. You weren't exactly discouraging just now.'

'I know. And I'm not proud of it. But it won't be happening again.' She thrust the cup and saucer forward. 'Will you please take this before I drop it?'

He did so, seizing her wrist with his free hand before she could withdraw, and jerking her forward on to the bed. The cup and saucer he deposited on his own bedside table with scant regard for the liquid slopped over.

'Don't ever start something you're not prepared to finish,' he advised. 'Not with me, anyway.'

She fought him furiously as he came over her. Only when he took both wrists and pinned them back to the pillows above her head did she desist, breath coming hard and heavy as she gazed up into the ruthless face.

'That's better,' he said. 'Just hold it there and you'll not get hurt.' Kneeling astride her, he ran his eyes down to her breasts, clearly outlined against the straining material. A small, grim smile touched his lips. 'The spirit may have developed cold feet, but the flesh still knows what it wants. Give me one good reason why I shouldn't satisfy us both?'

'The same reason you didn't send for the police,' she got out with an effort. 'Because you need me. If you rape me, Ryan...'

His laugh was short. 'Who said anything about rape?'

'I did.' She forced herself to lie still, aware that any further movement could only prove inflammatory. 'That's what it's going to take.'

'You wouldn't,' he said softly, 'like to take a bet on it?'

She wouldn't have bet a penny, but she couldn't afford to let him know that. 'If you go on with this,' she returned with intent, 'I'll be on the next available plane back to Heathrow.'

He studied her for a long moment, an odd expression in his eyes. 'I really think you mean that,' he said at length. 'Why the change, Kim? You weren't just ready back there, you were willing.'

'I was overwhelmed by your expertise,' she came back with self-directed irony. 'I realise you're unaccustomed to being turned down, Ryan, but they say a change is as good as a rest.'

Anger fought with humour for a brief moment, the latter winning by a short head. 'You,' he declared, 'are a one-off!'

The heat and weight of him across her thighs was no aid to resolve. She scarcely knew whether to be glad or sorry when he shifted away from her. Sitting up, she turned her back on him to reach for her coffee-cup with a hand that trembled. She had won because he had let her win; why, she still wasn't sure.

That question was answered for her when he spoke, his tone meaningful. 'Don't run away with the idea that this ends it. I'm going to make you eat every word before we're through!'

She made no reply to that; chiefly because she could think of nothing to say. Determination was all very well, but if he made another concerted effort she doubted her ability to stick to her guns. Going home was a solution to be considered with care. Made a fool and liar of before his mother and stepfather, he was bound to retaliate.

The closing of the bathroom door removed the immediate problem. Kim finished her coffee, and forced a piece of toast down an unwilling throat before getting up to start sorting out her things. A covering wrap was her first priority. Swanning around in a semi-transparent nightdress was hardly scheduled to improve matters.

She caught sight of her face in the dressing-table mirror as she filled one of the drawers beneath, faintly surprised to find it unaltered from its familiar lines. Not unattractive, she knew, yet not the kind of looks she would have thought likely to give Ryan Bentley any restless moments either, considering his more usual tastes. The situation itself had to be the biggest turn-on. How many men with normal male appetites could share a bed with a woman and remain absolutely detached?

The view from the window was rural in the extreme. Snow-laden pine trees crowded the boundary fences. Immediately below lay a substantial wooden veranda built out from the rear of the house and complete with what might be a covered hot tub, and beyond that again the unmistakable shape of a covered swimming-pool. There was no sign of any neighbouring houses, although there had certainly been other lights visible last night.

She was sufficiently in command of herself to meet the grey eyes without flinching when he emerged. Dressed once again in a low-slung towel, he was freshly

shaved and emotively scented. Kim managed to stop
her glance from wandering down over the fine, taut
body, but no amount of discipline could still the leap
in her pulse-rate, or unravel the knot in her stomach.
To make love—real love—with such a man would be
wonderful, but it would mean little beyond the immediate enjoyment to him. She had to keep re-
minding herself of that fact.

'How about lunch downtown?' he asked, sur-
prising her again because it was the last thing she
would have expected. 'I could show you something
of the city afterwards.'

'Your mother said Eloise would be here this afternoon,' she reminded him, thrusting the temptation to
the back of her mind. 'We can hardly just take off
for the day.'

'She'll still be here when we get back.' He was
turned away from her, opening a drawer to extract
clean underwear and socks—he must, Kim thought
irrelevantly, have unpacked last night while she was
taking a shower. 'We don't have to stand on any
ceremony.'

'All the same . . .' she began, her voice petering out
as he slanted her a hardened glance.

'Just leave it, will you?'

Shrugging, she took up her own things and went
into the bathroom. Whatever the reason for his obvious reluctance to meet his stepsister, it was nothing
to do with her. She had enough to think about without
that.

A thin-featured woman wearing a white overall was
dusting the hall furniture when they went down. Ryan
introduced her as Mrs Carson. She lived in the village,

Kim gathered, and had been the Dubois' daily house-keeper for the past five years. Her curiosity over the supposed new addition to the family was unconcealed.

Mike had already left. Seated in the breakfast alcove over a fresh cup of coffee, Kim listened while mother and son chatted in seemingly random fashion. His announcement of their plans for the day brought little comment, but there was no mistaking the dissension in the former's expression.

'You'll be back for dinner, I hope?' she said. 'I was planning something extra special to welcome Eloise home again. A lovely young woman,' she added to Kim with emphasis. 'We're very close.'

'I'm looking forward to meeting her,' Kim answered, not entirely truthfully. Eloise Dubois was a complication she could well do without.

They took the Cadillac to drive into town. Warm and comfortable, Kim looked out on the snow-covered landscape flanking the freeway, and wished she could be making this visit under rather more favourable conditions. There was so much she would have liked to see while she was here: Ottawa, Quebec itself, the Laurentians. To ski in the latter would be terrific, but there wasn't going to be much chance in a week.

Ryan drove the way he did everything, with pro-ficiency and skill yet without ostentation. His hands on the wheel gave her a sense of security totally at odds with other emotions he aroused. She was vi-brantly aware of the sheer animal magnetism of the man, recalling with dry throat the feel of him up close. Plain chemical reaction, she told herself, but she knew it was more than just that. Against every instinct of self-preservation, she was becoming emotionally involved. And there was no future in it.

While less spectacular than Manhattan, the Montreal skyline looked superb against the clear blue backdrop. Ryan took her first to Mount Royal to get an overall view of the city and river spread out below in panoramic splendour. Underneath all that, he said, lay miles of arcades and malls reached via the city's metro system, so that even in the severest weather conditions life still carried on as usual.

There were skaters on the frozen Beaver Lake. Some people, Ryan said, took advantage of their lunch break.

'Talking of which,' he added, 'I think we'd better find somewhere to thaw out before you turn completely blue!'

'I'm just not used to this degree of cold,' Kim responded wryly, trying to stop her teeth from chattering. 'Especially round the feet!'

'Remiss of me,' he agreed, casting a glance at her shoes. 'We'd better get you some warm boots after we've eaten. You're going to need them back out at Hudson, anyway.'

Kim was glad to get back to the car. Even wrapped as she was in fur, she felt chilled to the marrow. It was difficult to believe right now that summers here could bring temperatures in the high seventies.

He took her to a restaurant in the old quarter just off the Place Jacques Cartier. Converted from one of the lovely old Quebec houses, it was small and exclusive and, from what Kim could gather from a brief look at the menu, hideously expensive. She left it to Ryan to choose what they were to eat, sitting back to wriggle her toes in relief at their returning warmth. She had boots at home she could have brought with her, but it somehow hadn't occurred to her.

'Better?' he asked as the waiter departed with their order. 'At least your colour's good. When the nose turns white, that's the time to start worrying. The only thing then is to rub it in the snow.'

Kim found herself responding to the teasing note in his voice, so far removed from the mockery he usually displayed. 'I'll bear it in mind,' she promised. There was a momentary pause during which she found it impossible to tear her gaze away from the grey eyes. It was in sheer desperation that she tagged on, 'I had difficulty following you just now. Is the French spoken here different?'

'It's provincial,' he agreed. 'Takes a little practice.'

'So you have spent a fair amount of time over here, then?'

He shrugged. 'Up until the last year or so I commuted fairly regularly, yes.'

'Pressure of work?' she hazarded. 'That stopped you, I mean.'

'Something like that.' The quizzical look had vanished, replaced by the stoniness she was coming to know and dread. 'Would you like some wine?'

Kim murmured agreement, wryly aware of having trodden on forbidden ground. For a moment or two she had been on the verge of achieving a breakthrough to another Ryan Bentley lacking the sardonic edge of the first. That Eloise Dubois had something to do with his staying away from Montreal was in no doubt. The question was, what? Even if Lydia had

made her hopes for the two of them obvious, he could
surely have handled it.

Unless Eloise herself was the disinterested party,
came the thought. That would explain quite a lot.
Viewing the prospect, Kim couldn't deny the swift
pang in the region of her heart. The totally inviolate
male was somehow more preferable to one suffering
from unrequited love.

## CHAPTER FIVE

IT WAS gone three when they finally left the city after purchasing a pair of luxuriously warm and not too unflattering boots on Ste-Catherine Street. Ryan had also insisted on a thickly quilted parka which could be worn with trousers, as the one she had brought with her was quite inadequate. Returning those was obviously going to prove impossible, Kim reflected on the way back to Hudson, but she had no intention of keeping them either. They were simply props to use for the duration.

Snow began to fall as they neared the freeway exit. Gentle at first, it was coming thick and fast by the time they reached the house. Mike wasn't yet home, but a low-slung coupé now occupied the garage. Ryan passed it by without a glance.

Lydia and her stepdaughter awaited them in the sitting-room. Tall, like her father, the latter had jet-black hair cut to frame a set of near-perfect features. Dressed simply and casually in a plain brown skirt and sweater, her only embellishment a bright little scarf knotted about her throat, she still made Kim feel like some country cousin.

The greeting she offered Ryan was as expressionless as his own. Introduced, Kim was treated to a swift and narrowed appraisal of dark eyes.

'You look a lot younger than twenty-six,' Eloise commented. 'I hear you dabble in computers?'

Unless her looks were deceptive, she was no more than that herself, Kim reflected. Aloud she said drily, 'Something like that. Did you drive all the way from Ottawa?'

The smile had an edge. 'It beats walking. Lucky you got back before the weather closed in. *Marâtre* didn't get her snow-tyres fixed yet.'

The French for stepmother was the same, at least, Kim thought fleetingly, although the use of it seemed a trifle pretentious. There was, admittedly, rather more of the Gallic inheritance in Eloise than in her father.

'I'm sure Ryan would have handled it,' she returned with tongue tucked firmly into cheek. 'He could handle anything on wheels!'

'And off them.' The lenient note was belied by the glint in his eyes. 'Who's going to join me in a drink?'

All in the one glass? she almost asked, but thought better of it. His mood at the moment was not geared towards appreciation of unsubtle humour—if it ever was. About to join Lydia in opting out of the invitation, she abruptly changed her mind. Alcohol might infuse a little more confidence to carry her through what promised to be an ordeal of an evening: the hostility in Eloise's eyes had not been imagined.

'I'll have a straight vodka, please,' she requested, and steeled herself against the glance Ryan turned her way. There were times when sherry just wasn't enough.

Eloise moved to the black-lacquered drinks cabinet ahead of him. 'I'll fix my own,' she said coolly over a shoulder as he came up behind her.

From where she sat, Kim saw him make some comment, but his tone was too low for the words themselves to be audible. Eloise shrugged, and continued to mix her drink, her back unyielding. Catching Lydia's eye, Kim forced a smile.

'I hope Mike doesn't find himself snowbound. It seems to be coming down faster.'

'If he heard the noon forecast, he should be here any time,' came the reply. 'It's going to be blizzard conditions in a couple of hours.'

The wind was already rising; Kim could hear it in the trees. Driving through a snowstorm was hardly to be recommended, but Mike must know what he was doing. This was his country; he was used to the winter hazards.

Eloise had gone to take a seat on the sofa opposite. Ryan brought across the vodka Kim had asked for, parking himself casually on the arm of her chair to take a swallow from his own glass. One arm lay along the back; she could feel the material of his shirt-sleeve touching the hair at her nape.

Quite deliberately, she turned her head to lightly brush her cheek against his arm, gaining a reaction in the sudden tautening of the other girl's lips. What Ryan himself thought of the gesture she had no idea and, at that moment, didn't particularly care. One thing she refused to do was sit here playing mug-in-the-middle of whatever it was that was going on with these two.

Eloise's attitude altered completely when her father arrived some ten minutes or so later. The kiss with which she greeted him was composed enough, but there was no doubting the genuine warmth of her regard.

'Thank God it's the weekend!' he said when he too was comfortably seated with a drink to hand. 'We'll need the blower out to clear the drive again in the morning. It's drifting badly. You might like to give Cass a ride on the Skidoo some time,' he added to his stepson. 'Best way of seeing the area this time of year.'

'Skidoo?' Kim queried.

It was Ryan who answered. 'A kind of motorised scooter on skis. Not to be recommended to any but the foolhardy.'

Mike laughed. 'Not when my daughter drives it, for sure! I remember that time last winter she took you pillion and you both finished up to your necks in a drift. Lucky you were able to dry off at the Seguins' place, or you'd have been a couple of icicles before you got back here!'

Eloise's eyes were on Ryan, her expression set. 'I've learned caution since then,' she said.

And what had Ryan learned? wondered Kim hollowly, sensitive to the nuances in that ostensibly straightforward statement. There was more to their relationship than she had first imagined, for certain; the evidence was right there in front of her.

The blizzard was still raging when the household retired to bed for the night. Preceding Ryan into the room they shared, Kim waited until the door was closed before venting her feelings the only way she knew how.

'You might at least have warned me!'

'About what?' he asked, not moving from the door.

She spun to face him, trembling all over with an emotion too intense to be examined too closely. 'Don't take me for a complete fool!'

'That,' he said levelly, 'is one thing I'd never take you for. If you've something to say, get on with it.'

'You and Eloise.' She could barely get the words out. 'She's the one, isn't she?'

The grey eyes didn't flicker. 'Depends on what we're talking about exactly,' he returned. 'Spell it out for me.'

Kim paused to collect herself, conscious of the need to stay on top of her emotions. 'You were ... involved with her, weren't you?' she said stiffly.

'That's one way of putting it.' He still wasn't giving anything away. 'And, having ascertained that much, let's leave it right there.'

She stood her ground determinedly. 'I think I have a right to know just what I'm being used for. You said it was your mother who kept on at you to get married. Was it only her?'

A muscle tautened in the firm jawline. 'It makes no difference.'

'It does to me,' she said. 'You must have given them both good reason to believe it possible.'

His smile was grim. 'Where women are concerned, there's no such thing as reason. I'm not prepared to discuss it with you—now or any other time.'

'If you don't,' she threatened recklessly, 'I'll ask Eloise herself!'

He reached her in a stride, seizing a handful of hair to drag her head back so that she was looking straight into the steely eyes. 'Try it,' he gritted, 'and I'll make you sorrier than you've ever been!'

His grip on her hurt, but she wasn't about to show it. She saw his expression slowly alter, the anger give way to something less easily defined. When he spoke again, his tone was low and rough. 'Don't push me, Cass. I'm having enough trouble squaring my conscience as it is.'

If he had called her by her proper name instead of the hated alias, she might have been prepared to soften her attitude a little, but the bitter resentment flaring in her allowed no such deflection.

'You don't have a conscience,' she accused. 'You use people, Ryan! I might have done wrong myself trying to set things right for Tony, but it was at least an honest crime.'

The familiar mockery was back in his eyes. 'That's a contradiction in terms, darling. And, whatever the situation where Eloise is concerned, it has nothing to do with anyone else. That includes Mother, Mike *and* you. Clear enough?'

He didn't bother waiting for an answer. Kim swallowed thickly as he let go of her and turned away. That glimpse she had had this afternoon of a more empathetic personality had been nothing but an illusion. He was totally indifferent to the finer aspects of the human character.

Emerging from the bathroom later to see him already in bed, she knew a sudden desperation. Hate the man or not, her body still reacted to the thought of being close to him.

Her wrap was thin, but the room was warm enough. Switching out the light, she made her way across to one of the two easy chairs and settled herself down with a cushion tucked behind her head. Hardly an ideal way to spend a night, but preferable to the alternative.

Whole minutes passed with no sound but the whistling of the wind to break the silence, and that itself muted by the triple-glazing of the windows. Ryan's move to sit up jerked every nerve in her body.

'What the hell do you think you're doing?' he clipped. 'Get on over here.'

Kim found her voice with an effort. 'I don't trust you.'

'Me,' he queried with irony, 'or yourself?'

There was no point in denying it, she thought wryly. He was only too well aware of his power. 'All right, so I don't trust myself either,' she said, and hoped he wouldn't hear the faint quiver in her voice. 'I want to be able to live with myself after all this is over.'

He was silent for so long that she was almost beginning to think he had fallen asleep. When he did speak again it was with an odd inflexion. 'I'll leave you alone. Just get into bed.'

She said softly, 'I don't believe you.'

'Not even if I give you my word?'

'No.' It was strange talking like this in the darkness. She could hear her own heartbeats. 'Your word hasn't proved much of a guarantee up to now.'

'I suppose you're right at that,' he acknowledged. 'I didn't appreciate how difficult it was going to be at the time. You're a temptress, Kim. You challenge a man to prove himself. I want to make love to you. Is that such a bad thing?'

Her voice was husky. 'What you're talking about isn't making love. Not the way I see it. I'm not denying the way you can make me feel; I don't doubt you could do the same for any woman. Only I'm not just any woman. For me there has to be something more than just physical arousal.'

His smile was more sensed than seen. 'You mean you'd have to be in love with a man before you could indulge your natural instincts without feeling dissolute? That's an outdated concept.'

'Where the kind of women you're more used to dealing with are concerned, very probably,' she retorted. 'Love is a meaningless word to you, isn't it, Ryan?'

'Judging from the divorce rate, it doesn't have any lasting meaning to many,' he came back drily. 'I simply prefer to keep my options open until I meet someone I could contemplate spending the rest of my life with. What's so wrong with that?'

The cynicism came too easily. 'Does such a paragon exist?'

'Hopefully.' There was a pause, a faint sigh. 'Look, I meant what I said. I shan't touch you. Not unless you force me to come over there and fetch you, that is.'

If he did, there was no knowing what might happen, Kim conceded, feeling the treacherous lurch of her pulses. She got reluctantly to her feet and crossed the floor, sliding between the sheets with as little disturbance as she could manage, to lie on her back staring up at the dim ceiling.

Ryan lay down again himself, careful to retain the width of the bed between them. 'Go to sleep,' he said gruffly. 'You don't have a thing to worry about.'

It was what she had wanted, so why, Kim asked herself, this feeling of utter deflation? She had to practise what she preached—didn't she?

Ryan had gone from the bed when she awoke at eight. Only on sitting up did she become aware of the lack of wind noise from outside. The scene from the window was one of pure, sparkling splendour, with every tree laden in white beneath a sky of cobalt-blue. All sign of the swimming-pool had vanished beneath the covering mantle, while the drifts up against the boundary fence had to be several feet deep.

No climate for the faint at heart, Kim acknowledged, trying to imagine what conditions must be like in the open. The cold might be healthy, but several months of it would tax even the most indomitable spirit.

Dressed in beige cord trousers and toning sweater, she went downstairs to find Mrs Carson alone in the kitchen. Both men were outside with the blower clearing the front drive, it appeared. Lydia and Eloise had gone down to the village on the Skidoo.

'Want me to fix you some breakfast?' the woman asked as Kim stood hesitantly in the doorway. 'There's plenty of coffee still in the pot.'

'I'll just make myself some toast,' she responded. 'That's all I normally have.'

The shrug was easy. 'Suit yourself.'

She went back to work wiping down the kitchen surfaces, leaving Kim to find bread and slot a couple of slices into the toaster. The coffee-pot had its own hotplate. Pouring a cup, she took it and her plate through the archway to the beamed and boarded breakfast area. The Dubois were obviously early risers, which made her feel very tardy. Guests who lounged around in bed half the morning were never popular.

She wasn't just an ordinary guest though, was she? she reminded herself. Not on the face of it. As Ryan's 'wife' she could afford to take a few liberties. Sitting here now, she wished herself anywhere else. There were at least four more days to get through before she could start thinking of home. She wasn't sure she could last the course.

'Never thought Mr Ryan would finally go and do it,' remarked Mrs Carson from beyond the partition. 'Not the marrying type, I'd have said.'

'Would you?' Kim answered politely. 'It just goes to show how wrong impressions can be.'

'That's right.' The woman paused, her tone altering a fraction. 'You're not what any of them expected either.'

That Kim could readily believe. Georgina, Chloe, Eloise—all of them very different types, and none of them anything like her. Of the three of them, it was only Eloise who bothered her at all. The others were just passing fancies. Not that she had any grounds for jealousy anyway.

The opening of the rear porch door stemmed any further overtures on Mrs Carson's part. The two men sloughed boots and thick jackets before coming on through to the warmth. Meeting the steady grey eyes, Kim felt a flush creep into her cheeks. The memory of last night's conversation was too sharp and clear in her mind for dispassionate encounter.

'You should have woken me,' she said, trying for a light note. 'I could have helped clear the snow.'

'And frozen solid in the process,' joked Mike, blowing on his hands. 'It's ten below and still dropping out there.'

'Lydia and Eloise don't seem to mind it,' she remarked.

'They're dressed for it, and used to it. The village is only a couple of miles away. You'll have to pay a visit yourself. Come the summer, we'll take a trip out to Matane. That's where I was born. The whole peninsula's worth seeing.'

'That would be nice,' she agreed, realising some comment was necessary and feeling a total fraud. Come the summer, she and Ryan would have supposedly separated. That they would have in reality too made things no better.

Ryan slid along the bench seat to join her, a mug of coffee in his hand. He was wearing a white cable-knit sweater that made his hair look even darker by contrast. Thick and springy, the latter gleamed with health and vitality.

'We'll go for a walk this afternoon,' he said. 'Try out the new boots.'

'Why not take the skis?' Mike suggested. 'Should be good going.' He looked enquiringly at Kim. 'That's taking it you can use skis?'

'I've done some,' she said. 'Not a lot on the flat, though.'

'Great way to get around. Good exercise too.' He patted his midriff with a grin. 'Could do with some myself, if it comes to that, but I'll settle for a nap by the fire instead. There's a good big one lit through in the den, if you're interested.'

With central heating this efficient, Kim could see no need of a fire at all, but she could appreciate the attraction of leaping flames. She made the appropriate response.

'Talking of skiing,' Mike went on, 'we're planning on spending Christmas up at the Lodge. Be nice if the two of you came with us.'

Kim looked up sharply. 'I don't really think——'

'It might be an idea,' Ryan cut in. His tone was easy, expression equally so. 'It's more than three years since I was up there.'

'We have to get back,' she said, hoping she didn't sound as impassioned as she felt. 'My job——'

'You're not due to start the new one until the New Year.' Ryan was smiling, but his eyes held a warning. 'We'd still be back before then.'

'So we can take that as settled?' Mike sounded gratified. 'Lydia will be delighted.'

Would Eloise? wondered Kim. She hid her simmering anger behind a bright smile, avoiding Ryan's gaze for fear she might give the whole game away. She was as guilty as he was in allowing things to go so far. The thought of facing exposure now was more than she could contemplate.

The two women arrived back looking like eskimos in their fur-lined parkas. One of their neighbours had tried to drive down to the village, and flattened the battery trying to get the car started again after skidding into a drift, Lydia said. Would Mike take the jump leads down and get her out?

Ryan went with him. Feeling distinctly the outsider, Kim offered to help the other two to put away the purchases they had made. Refusal on the grounds that she wouldn't know where things belonged made sense, she supposed, but it didn't make her any the less uncomfortable. Eloise in particular seemed intent on cold-shouldering her.

'I'm going up to change before we start lunch,' Lydia announced when everything was tidy again. 'The menfolk should be back by the time I get down. Why don't you two go and have coffee in the den?' she added. 'The fire's lit.'

Eloise shrugged, turning an expressionless glance in Kim's direction. 'Would you like some coffee?'

Already awash with the stuff, but with nothing better to do at the moment, Kim nodded. 'Please.'

Wood-panelled, and furnished as a cross between study, library and sitting-room, the den was off the far side of the hall. A wide stone fireplace held a blazing pile of logs. Seated in one of the deep and supremely comfortable leather armchairs, with a view of the snow-covered landscape through floor to ceiling windows, she had to admit that central heating could never rival the real thing.

'We used to have open fires at home when I was a child,' she said to the silent figure on the other side of the fireplace, trying to find some way of breaking through the barriers. 'They always fascinated me because of all the pictures the embers seem to form. They still do.'

'Where did you and Ryan meet?' Eloise asked, ignoring the overture.

Caught short, Kim tried to remember what Ryan had told her to say, but her mind was blank. 'At a party,' she hazarded. She tried a smile, lightening her tone. 'Across a crowded room, and all that!'

Dark brows lifted expressively. 'It was love at first sight?'

'Oh, completely!' Not for anything, Kim told herself, was she going to reveal the true state of her

nerves at this point. If she had to put on an act, let
it be a good one. She found a laugh. 'Knowing Ryan,
can you blame me for falling for him?'

The answer was a moment or two coming, the
other's eyes registering a certain inner struggle. When
she did speak, it was on a note of some reluctance.
'No, I don't blame you. I felt much the same myself
the first time I saw him.' She paused, assessing Kim's
reaction with a grim little smile. 'He didn't tell you
about us, did he?'

Kim shook her head, not sure how to handle this
unexpected development. 'I rather gathered there
might have been something a bit deeper than a sister-
brother relationship between you,' she said hesitantly. 'But nothing that happened before I met him
is really my affair.'

'A *bit* deeper?' The laugh was harsh. 'We were
lovers!'

Kim closed her eyes for a moment, the better to
absorb the shock. Somehow, she had never imagined
matters might have gone as far as that. 'You shouldn't
be telling me all this,' she got out.

'Why not?' Eloise asked bitterly. 'You should know
the kind of man you married. The kind who takes
what he wants from a woman then discards her the
same way he'd discard an automobile! Marriage isn't
going to change him. Nothing can change him. If you
take my advice, you'll make sure you have a good
lawyer standing by for when the time comes that he
wants out. And it will come. Once the novelty of
having a wife wears off, he'll want his freedom back.'

Hell hath no fury, Kim reminded herself hollowly.
The old adage was certainly being borne out here.

'Ryan hasn't lost any freedom,' she said with what steadiness she could muster. 'Marriage isn't a strait-jacket.'

'You're trying to tell me you wouldn't care if he had other women?'

'Of course I'd care. I'd hope and trust it wouldn't happen, but there's no guarantee. If he does feel the need for other women it will be failure on my part as much as on his.' And that, Kim thought disgustedly, was the biggest load of rubbish she'd ever trotted out!

From the way Eloise was looking at her, the opinion was shared. 'You're more tolerant than I'd be in your shoes,' she said.

Kim forced herself to try and view this whole affair objectively. What Eloise was doing, in effect, was providing a foundation for Ryan's planned separation. He should be delighted. In the meantime, all *she* had to do was keep up the pretence.

'But you're not in my shoes,' she said. 'And I'd as soon stop this conversation.'

The sculptured features took on a look of disdain. 'You'll learn.'

Nothing she hadn't already learned, came the hollow reflection. Brilliant in business though he might be, as a human being Ryan Bentley left a lot to be desired.

## CHAPTER SIX

LYDIA, it turned out, took the same size as Kim in footwear. Wearing the new parka, Kim shouldered a pair of the narrower and lighter cross-country skis and joined Ryan on the drive. The snow cleared by the portable blower earlier was piled four feet deep either side, creating a passage. The air was crisp and cold, but in the absence of wind not unbearable. Exhilarating was the word which sprang to Kim's mind.

Hard-packed by the passage of vehicles, the road surface formed an excellent base for the skis. They moved in tandem, striking off into the trees at the junction with the village road. Apart from the swish of the runners and the occasional thud as a branch gave up part of its load, all was silent. Difficult to think that the province's largest city was only an hour's drive away, Kim reflected, enjoying the isolation. It was like stepping into another world.

They weren't the only ones with the same idea. Twice, they crossed tracks left by other skiers. Aware of the necessity to say what had to be said, yet reluctant to mar the afternoon, she waited until Ryan stopped to take a breather in a small clearing before giving voice.

'You promised me this was only going to be for a week at the longest. Staying over Christmas wasn't part of the bargain.'

Broad shoulders lifted. 'It wasn't part of the original plan, but I could hardly turn it down. It may be the last Christmas my mother sees.'

'You mean you've actually developed a sense of duty?' Kim made no effort to play down the scepticism. 'Better late than never, I suppose, but it still doesn't alter the fact that I'm expected home for Christmas.'

He said drily, 'I doubt if your brother is going to pine away for need of companionship. Not from what I understood of his lifestyle.'

Blue eyes sharpened. 'You checked up on him?'

'I thought I was entitled to know a bit more about an employee who'd had his fingers in the till. Quite the Lothario, by all accounts. Considering his taste for the gambling table, I'm surprised he was only in for a thousand.'

'It was the first time he'd done any serious gambling,' she returned swiftly. 'The people he owed the money to were threatening him with physical injury if he didn't pay up within a couple of days. That's the only reason he stooped to crime.'

'Well, let's hope he learned his lesson. Next time big sister may not be able to help him out.'

'There won't be a next time.' Her tone was stony. 'And you're avoiding the issue. You deliberately put me in a position where I can't insist on leaving as planned without appearing in a bad light.'

'It wouldn't do you any good anyway,' he returned. 'If I stay we both stay.' He straightened, using both sticks to propel himself forward. 'Let's go.'

With no idea of the way back, Kim had no other recourse but to follow the tall, black-jacketed figure.

His attitude should come as no shock, she acknowledged grimly. Ryan Bentley went his own way regardless. At least he was showing some concern for
his mother's health and well-being. After all, he had
plenty to get back to himself. Chloe, for one, wasn't
going to be best pleased by his continued absence from
the social circle they obviously shared.

They emerged from the tree cover shortly afterwards to follow the line of a fence enclosing the
grounds of a large, single-storeyed house.

'Closed up for the winter,' Ryan explained when
Kim commented on the depth of virgin show at the
front premises. 'The Seguins spend several months
every year at their place down in Florida. Mike keeps
an eye on the house for them—runs the furnace, et
cetera.'

Seguin. The same name Mike had mentioned yesterday when describing the Skidoo incident, Kim re-
called. Yet if the people themselves hadn't been here
at the time...

'I gather Eloise just happened to have the key with
her when you came off the bike that afternoon?' she
said with deliberation, drawing a sudden narrowing
of the grey eyes as he glanced her way.

'As a matter of fact, yes. She'd been in to check
for mail delivery that same morning.'

'How fortuitous. And the Seguins didn't mind you
using their facilities?'

'I don't suppose they ever knew, but no, they
wouldn't have minded. Canadians are a hospitable
race.' Ryan rested his weight on the planted sticks, a
line drawn between his brows. 'What are you getting
at?'

Her shrug was over-casual. 'What *would* I be getting at?'

'Never answer a question with another question,' he advised. 'It just points to prevarication. Now supposing we stop playing games?'

She drew in a shallow breath of the cold air, already feeling the effects of the lowering temperature as the afternoon moved towards early evening. 'Shouldn't we be getting back?' she asked. 'It must be quite a distance.'

'No more than half a mile. We've been heading in a circular direction.' He made no move, eyes penetrating her defences. 'We'll stand here till you start explaining—if we freeze to the spot!'

Her chin lifted, her gaze defiant. 'All right, then, is this where it started with you two, or was that the time you realised she was getting too serious about you?'

The expression which crossed the lean features was too swiftly come and gone for accurate assessment. 'Where what started?'

Her laugh came short and sharp. 'You should follow your own advice!' She watched his mouth tauten ominously, and knew she had gone too far to back out now. Not that she wanted to back out. 'Eloise told me,' she stated flatly. 'You hurt her, Ryan.'

His tone was surprisingly restrained. 'Does this really have anything to do with you?'

'You made me a part of it yourself,' she retorted. 'I'm entitled to a viewpoint.' She drew in another harsh breath. 'I'd have thought even you would draw the line at your stepsister!'

'Why?' he asked. 'There's no blood tie.' This time
the anger was only just held in check. 'She's a full-
grown woman, in case you hadn't noticed.'

'That's totally irrelevant!' Kim was too incensed to
heed the danger signals. 'You just don't give a damn
who gets hurt, do you, Ryan, so long as you get what
*you* want? I only hope you get a taste of your own
medicine some time, although I doubt if you're
capable of feeling anything for anyone deeply enough
for it to happen!'

'Finished?' he asked silkily as she paused for breath.
'Or was there something else you wanted to add?'

It was useless trying to get through that hide of his,
she conceded. She might just as well save her breath.
There was scorn in the look she gave him, hiding the
deeper, less worthy emotion he conjured in her even
now. 'Why bother?'

He turned without another word and headed for
the narrow line of the road. Kim followed, turning
left to his right on reaching it, and digging in her sticks
with a steadily mounting fury to drive herself forward
at a pace she knew she couldn't keep up for long.

She had gone no more than a few hundred yards
when he caught up with her. Passing her, he executed
a side-slip to bring himself block in front of her. His
eyes were glittering, his whole face grimly set.

'What the devil is this supposed to prove?' he
clipped.

She steadied herself with both sticks, too angry still
to care. 'I'd as soon find my own way back, thanks!'

'You'd be a long time doing it in this direction—if
ever.' He made a visible effort to bring his own temper

under control, breath coming harshly. 'I've no need of an overseer!'

'I despise you!' Her voice tremored with emotional conflict. 'I really despise you, Ryan!'

His lips twisted. 'That's unfortunate, because you're still going to have to spend the next ten days with me, like it or not. Turn around, darling.'

Short of knocking him out with a swing of a ski stick, there was nothing she could do but obey the injunction. Biting her lip, she swung herself about and moved off ahead of him. The worst part of this whole affair, she admitted painfully, was the way he could make her feel deep down inside. She could tell herself he wasn't worth it till the cows came home, but it made little difference to her senses.

As he had said, they were within half a mile of the house. They stacked the skis in the garage to be re-waxed, and changed into the ordinary shoes they'd left ready in the side lobby before going through to the kitchen where Mrs Carson was preparing vegetables for the evening meal.

'Had a good run?' she enquired cheerfully. 'You'll be ready for a hot drink, I'd guess. Mrs Dubois said to wait tea till you got back.'

The last thing Kim felt like was making small talk over a cup of tea, but from the expression on Ryan's face as their glances clashed she wasn't to be allowed any escape. Ten more days of this was going to seem like a lifetime!

They found Lydia and Mike in the den. Eloise, it appeared, had gone to visit friends.

'There's more snow forecast tomorrow,' Mike advised. 'The *pistes* should be good this year. We're planning on driving up Thursday, by the way. Hélène and Yves are delighted you're going to be spending Christmas.'

So it wasn't to be just a family affair, thought Kim hollowly. That made it even worse. 'How many will be there altogether?' she asked.

'Around thirty, including the Lemoynes themselves,' Lydia supplied. 'Not that they'll have too much free time with the hotel to run.' She paused, viewing Kim's expression in sudden realisation. 'You thought we kept another home going up there?'

Kim smiled and shrugged. 'It didn't seem all that far-out an idea. Plenty of people back home keep weekend cottages.'

'With the Lodge available any time we want to get away for a weekend, there's no need,' said Mike comfortably. 'The Lemoynes run the place like a home from home, anyway. You'll like them, Cass. They're good people. Christmas with them is like it used to be. No television, no commercialisation, just one big happy family gathering.'

'It sounds wonderful,' she said, and thought how true that would have been under other circumstances. It was years since she had spent a family Christmas.

Eloise telephoned through some time later to say she would be staying the night at her friend's home. Relieved of her presence at the dinner table, Kim found it easier to dissemble. Lydia herself had begun to unbend a little. What couldn't be altered had to be accepted, or at least endured, seemed to be her maxim. Given the opportunity, Kim considered, they might even have achieved a certain rapport one day.

Bedtime brought a return of restraint. It was getting harder, not easier, to share a room and bed with the man she both hated and lusted after at one and the same time. She went up ahead of him, and hurried through the rituals so that she could be in bed and ostensibly asleep when he did put in an appearance. Not that she anticipated any further approach from him. He had made it plain enough last night that his interest had cooled to the point of not caring.

She was in bed, but far from sleep when he arrived. As on that first night, she lay like a log listening to the sounds he made. When he slid between the sheets at last, she found herself holding her breath, letting it go on a sigh muffled by the back of her hand pressed against her lips. She could feel the heat of his body even at this distance, could imagine the rest. Imagining never did anyone any harm—did it?

The hand which turned her over on to her back was no figment of imagination. Neither was the feel of him against her, unhampered by clothing of any kind. Reflected by the snow outside, the moonlight outlined every detail of the strongly moulded features, turning his skin to alabaster, his eyes to twin sparks. His shoulders were a wide cloak, silvered along the upper edges.

'I told you we'd have to reach more than one kind of understanding before we were through,' he said on a low, rough note. 'And there's only one way we're going to do it.'

Repulsing him was the last thing on her mind at that moment, even if he'd been prepared to listen. She met his lips hungrily, giving free rein to the emotions running riot inside her. She was going to regret this for the rest of her life, came the fading thought, then that too was gone and there was only sensation.

He removed her nightdress with a practised expertise which might once have alienated her, but which now simply served a purpose her whole body craved. She trembled when he lifted himself up to look at her, half glad of the semi-darkness, half resenting it too.

The slow passage of his hand down over the curve of her waist and hipbone was exquisite. 'Smooth as silk,' he murmured, and splayed his fingers very gently across the fluttering skin of her abdomen, smiling at the sudden tension in her limbs. Then he was bending his head again to her breast, tongue like quicksilver on her heated skin, making her writhe beneath him like some demented creature.

He left scarcely a single inch of her untouched by those seeking, all-knowing lips of his, rousing her to fever pitch. Body on fire, limbs trembling, she found herself following where he led, tasting the faint saltiness of his skin from the light sheen of perspiration, stimulated to even greater lengths by the wiry tickle of his body hair. He was so taut, so powerful, so totally and completely the dominant male. His name filled her mind, his masculine scent her nostrils, his physical presence a gap she hadn't really known existed in her life to date. There was no call this time for the knee between her thighs. She was only too ready to respond to his every move, limbs supple as willows, hips lifting eagerly to meet him, the gasp drawn from her lips involuntary as their bodies joined, became one. Nothing could ever match this moment, this absolute realisation, came the thought before everything melted into one great, surging wave.

He stayed with her afterwards. Propped on his elbows, he put his lips to her temple where the hair clung damply. 'That,' he said softly, 'was worth waiting for!'

They had met on Tuesday; today was Saturday, Kim thought, coming back down to earth with a painful thud. Not exactly a long wait.

'I suppose,' she got out, 'I set up quite a record.'

His laugh came low. 'You're far from an easy conquest, if that's what's worrying you. We were both of us ready for this two days ago, but you wouldn't give in to it. True?'

She made no attempt to deny it; there was no point. The rapture had given way to shame, stark and raw. She was under no illusions about the man who held her in his arms. Nothing had changed. Self-indulgence at the cost of self-esteem, that was what it boiled down to.

'I want to go home,' she whispered, throat hurting. 'Please, Ryan . . .'

The denial came with flat intonation. 'You can't. Not yet. I need you.' He rolled away from her to lie on his back looking up at the ceiling, breath still coming heavily. 'It could be good, Kim. We only just got started. Why not enjoy it?'

'It isn't going to happen again.' She almost choked on the words. 'I don't *want* it to happen again!'

'Like hell you don't!' The humour was grim. 'Give me five minutes and I'll prove it to you!'

She turned her back on him, clinging to the bed-edge as a drowning man might clutch at a straw. Her voice was muffled by the pillow. 'Just leave me alone.'

There was a lengthy pause before he answered. The sigh held a note of resigned tolerance. 'Have it your own way. Only don't expect me to stay my own side of the bed for the duration. Not after the way you were just now. I don't have that kind of forbearance.'

She had no one to blame but herself, Kim acknowledged painfully. If she hadn't responded so wildly, he would have had no incentive to repeat the performance. There would be no response the next time; she'd make sure of it. See how long his interest lasted then!

He was still asleep when she slid from the bed at six-thirty. Showered, and dressed in a cream wool skirt and apricot sweater, she made her way down to the kitchen to make some coffee. It being Sunday, Mrs Carson wouldn't be coming in, and the rest of the family were unlikely to be around for another hour. Just to be alone for a while was a comfort of sorts.

Seated in the breakfast bay, she looked out on the clean-swept veranda and visualised the way it would be in the summer, with loungers and tables and a barbecue sending out delicious aromas. Canadians everywhere were lovers of the great outdoors, she had read. Sports enthusiasts too. Mike ski'd, fished, played golf like a professional, and brought home a trophy every time he went hunting, Ryan had told her. A man of action, for all his self-deprecation.

As if in response to her thoughts, the subject of them came into the kitchen. He was fully dressed in trousers and sweater, his jaw freshly shaved.

'Thought I heard somebody come down,' he said easily. 'Any of that going?'

'I made a potful,' Kim acknowledged. 'I hope you don't mind.'

The surprise was unassumed. 'Any reason why I should?'

'Lydia might object to having her kitchen invaded.'

Amusement widened his mouth. 'Lydia's not what you'd call kitchen-orientated. Sundays, we eat the main meal out. As family, this is as much your home now as anybody's, so you do just as you like.'

Guilt made her voice sound stilted. 'Thanks.'

Mike poured himself a cup of coffee, and brought it through to where she sat, taking a seat on the other side of the pine table. The eyes resting on her face were shrewd.

'Teething problems?' he asked.

She looked back at him blankly. 'I'm sorry?'

'It takes time,' he said, as if she hadn't spoken. 'No two people can adjust to living together without a few spats. Ryan's a great guy, but he's used to doing things his own way. Any man who waits till his age to get married is going to find the sharing tough. Stick with it, girl. He's worth it.'

She said softly, 'You're assuming I'm down here because we had a row?'

He shrugged. 'It was pretty obvious you'd been at each other's throats yesterday when you got back from the run, and you still hadn't gotten over it when you went up to bed.'

Kim made an attempt at a smile. 'I hadn't realised it showed so much. Anyway, everything is fine now.'

'Bed's the best place to sort things out,' came the tolerant agreement. 'Shows a man who's really in charge!'

How true, she thought with irony. Aloud, she said, 'Does Lydia realise the full extent of her condition, Mike, or aren't you telling her?'

He accepted the change of subject without a flicker. 'She knows.'

'It doesn't seem to affect her.'

'She won't let it,' he said. 'A strong woman, is my wife. It's a pity her heart isn't up to the rest of her.' Just for a moment there was an element of strain in his eyes. 'There's an op she could have, but the chances are only fifty/fifty of her coming out of it. Up to now, she says the odds don't attract her, though I suspect she's coming round to the idea. In the meantime, I just live in hope that she doesn't have another attack.' He paused, added sombrely, 'My first wife died from a heart attack when Eloise was twelve. Seems unfair, doesn't it, when mine just carries on going? The incidence of heart trouble in men is supposed to be far greater.'

'I'm sorry.' Kim could think of nothing better to say.

His smile was wry. 'Yes, well, that's the way it goes. At the very least, she's seen Ryan with a wife. With any luck, she may even make it to being a grandmother. Always taking it you do plan on having children?'

Kim hoped the flush didn't show. 'We didn't discuss it yet, but I imagine so.'

'Better sooner than later. Careers aren't everything.'

'Not for women, you mean?' She kept her tone light. 'I didn't have you down for a chauvinist, Mike.'

He grinned, mood successfully uplifted. 'Through and through! Not that Lydia goes in for much knee-bending, as you may have noticed. Comes from choosing a mate with the heart, not the head.'

It was hardly the time, but the words were out before Kim could stop them. 'She'd have liked Eloise as a daughter-in-law, wouldn't she? Did you feel the same way?'

'There might have been a time,' he admitted, 'but I realised it wasn't going to happen. Lydia clung to the hope against all the odds, that's all. You can't live your kids' lives for them, much as you'd sometimes like to.'

'And you don't blame Ryan?'

His brows lifted. 'Why blame Ryan? Having somebody fall for him puts him under no obligation to return the feeling. Eli wasted too much time waiting for him to see her as something more than a kid sister. It took his marriage to finally convince her. I'm glad to see her accepting it so well.'

Not always so perceptive, she thought as he lifted his cup to his lips. That he was unaware of the full extent of his daughter's involvement with his stepson was only too plain. God willing, he would never find out.

She tried to retain some measure of outer calm, at least when Ryan himself put in an appearance some minutes later. She was even able to meet the quizzical gaze without flinching. Listening to him talking with his stepfather, she wondered how he could face him after what he had done. No matter whether Eloise herself had instigated the affair; he was the guilty one in allowing it to happen at all. He hadn't even cared for the girl. Not in any way that counted. That was the worst part of all.

It was mid-afternoon before Eloise returned. They'd been skating up at Beaver Lake, she said. She was still wearing the outfit of thick tights and short-skirted red dress, her legs long and shapely. Kim saw Ryan run an eye over them and smile, fuming inwardly at the gall of the man. He had held Eloise in his arms the way he had held her last night, had made love to her with that same overriding passion. And none of it meant anything to him apart from the immediate gratification.

She turned down his invitation to take a look at the village via the Skidoo on the grounds that it was too cold. As the temperature had dropped several points from the same time yesterday, he accepted the refusal at face-value.

'You'll not mind if I go off on my own for a while, then?' he queried lightly. 'Sitting around doing nothing goes against the grain.'

'Feel free,' Kim responded, equally lightly. 'I didn't get through with the funnies yet.' Her smile was directed at Lydia. 'Your Sunday newspapers are more like a book!'

'Depends on the type of literature you're used to,' said Eloise on a sarcastic note. 'I'll come with you, Ryan.'

Whatever the latter's reactions to the offer, there was no telling from his expression. 'Fine,' he said. 'Providing I drive.'

She laughed, a suddenly heightened colour in her cheeks. 'It's entirely your choice. Just give me a few minutes to get changed.'

She was ready in less than five, hair tucked up beneath an emerald-green hat to match the polo-necked sweater, body swathed in sheepskin, feet shod in fur-lined boots. Her eyes were alive again, her whole attitude changed. Looking at her, Kim knew a sense of foreboding. She hadn't given up on Ryan. Not yet. Not ever, unless he made it clear there was nothing left between them.

Only was that really true? The expression on his face as he'd studied her a little while ago had hardly been one of total uninterest.

The two of them had been gone half an hour when the threatened snow began to fall. As neither Mike nor Lydia showed any particular concern, Kim could only assume that her fears of their becoming snow-bound were groundless. All the same, she couldn't relax until she heard the vehicle returning at last.

Eloise wore a recognisable air of satisfaction when they came into the den. The glance she directed at Kim was more than a little malicious.

'Glorious run!' she exclaimed. 'We went all the way through to Hudson.'

Hudson, or the Seguins' place? wondered Kim, meeting enigmatic grey eyes as Ryan lowered himself to a seat opposite. There was just no telling what went on in that dark head.

# CHAPTER SEVEN

THE snow had all but stopped by the time they set out for the small hotel patronised every Sunday when the Dubois were home. Small, but exclusive, Kim discovered without surprise.

The only language in use at the establishment appeared to be French. Hers was rusty enough without the disparities, but the menu was no problem. She chose the roast beef, disconcerted to find it reeking of garlic when it came.

'We should have warned you,' said Lydia. 'It's always done that way here. Why don't you choose something else?'

'Yes, do,' urged Ryan on a note calculated to raise Kim's hackles. 'There's nothing worse than second-hand garlic!'

'Eating it oneself is supposed to counteract it,' she returned levelly. 'I hate wasting good food.'

She saw his nostrils pinch as she took the first bite, and knew he had received the message. No lover of the pungent seasoning herself when used in quantity, she had to force the meat down her throat. Worth any sacrifice, she told herself, to keep him away from her tonight. Married or not, he would no doubt be welcomed by Eloise with open arms.

The latter was certainly more animated than she had been these past two days. Whatever the pair of them had said, or done, this afternoon, it had given her cause to think all was not lost. If she had been part of the reason Ryan had formulated this crazy idea, then he was hardly doing himself any favours by starting it up again. Not that he'd give a thought to Eloise's feelings either.

'If you've nothing pressing on the agenda for tomorrow,' Mike remarked casually over coffee, 'you might like to bring Cass in to the office. We just had a new computer system installed,' he added for her benefit. 'Be interesting to hear your opinion.'

This was hardly the time or place to start explaining the difference between program and system analysis, Kim acknowledged. 'I'd be interested to see it,' she said.

'That's settled, then.' He sounded pleased. 'Make it around eleven, then we can all lunch together. Gives you the afternoon for any shopping you want to do. They run a ski-hire shop up at St Justin, by the way, so you're not going to need too much in the way of equipment—although I guess you'll prefer your own suit.'

'I may join you,' Eloise put in blandly. 'I have some shopping to do myself.'

'Good idea.' Ryan sounded totally at ease. 'If I have to hit the stores, it may as well be with two women in tow as one.'

They had all five come down in the Lincoln, the two men up front. For the journey back, Ryan insisted his mother take the front passenger seat beside her husband, and he himself occupied the centre of the rear squab between the girls. In a car that size there was plenty of room for three without encroaching on each other's territory. With several inches separating her thighs from his, Kim wondered cynically if Eloise was out of touching distance too.

It was no more than a ten-minute drive back to the house. By nine o'clock they were all seated around the blazing fire in the den in various attitudes of relaxation. The television was turned on to catch the world news, then promptly turned off again to facilitate conversation. Drinks were poured.

Had everything been as it should be, she could have enjoyed an evening like this, Kim reflected, looking around the circle of faces lit by the flames. As it was, she had to be constantly on the alert. Twice she had failed to respond to her alias, drawing curious glances from Eloise if from no one else. It was getting more difficult rather than easier to carry the pretence through.

How Ryan could sit there untouched by any shadow of guilt, she failed to understand. The lies wouldn't finish when they left; there was still the supposed separation and eventual divorce to come. She would have no part in that, thank God! Once back home, she never wanted to see him again.

It was Ryan who made the first move towards breaking up the evening.

'Must be the air,' he said, smothering a yawn with the back of his hand. 'I've had it.' His eyes sought Kim's, devoid of all expression. 'Coming?'

The temptation to say no, and hope he was asleep before she went up, was strong, but she evaded it. Even though the garlic taste had disappeared, her breath would be far from sweet. The biggest turn-off there was, she had heard said.

It appeared to be working too, because he made no move towards her when they were alone in the bedroom.

'You go first, if you like,' he invited. 'I've one or two things to sort out.'

She didn't bother asking what. Once in the spacious, beautifully equipped bathroom, she swiftly stripped off her clothes and stepped under the shower, drawing the curtain across after her.

The water was hot, the jets adjustable to a needle spray that stimulated the skin. With her hair protected by a cap, she let the water play over her for several minutes after rinsing off the soap, enjoying the tingling sensation. Negative ions, she thought, lifting her face to the flow and feeling her spirits expand in accordance. She could handle this situation; she could handle *any* situation. Let Ryan do his worst!

The swish of the curtain at her back was the only warning she got. Twice the size of the average shower tray back home, the area provided plenty of room for Ryan to step in behind her. He was naked, she realised at once as he slid both arms about her waist and bent his lips to the side of her neck. But then, he would be, wouldn't he? He was hardly going to step under running water fully dressed!

The shocked suspension lasted bare seconds before giving way to a savage, white-hot fury. Under normal conditions, the foot she lashed back at his shin would have produced a fair amount of pain; as it was, she lost her balance on the wet base and would have fallen if he hadn't immediately drawn her closer up against him.

'You'll do yourself an injury,' his voice mocked at her ear.

Water blinding her, she gasped fiercely, 'I'll do *you* one first, you—you *degenerate*! Let go of me!'

'Not for a thousand dollars,' he retorted. 'You feel far too good.' Both hands came up to cup her breasts, thumbs caressing the already hardening nipples with a slow stroking motion that tore an involuntary whimper from her throat. Struggling only served to inflame matters. She forced herself to stand stock-still in his arms, lower lip caught between her teeth as she fought the treacherous emotion. No response, she reminded herself grimly. Let him do his worst!

Saying it was one thing, carrying it through something else again. Holding her to him with one hand, he allowed the other free rein of her body, exploring every line, every curve. She stiffened when the long, lean fingers slid across her abdomen to lightly brush the silky gold cluster, her breath sharply indrawn, but there was no denying the tumult of feeling he was releasing in her.

She went without protest when he turned off the water and drew her out into the bathroom. There was a hot darkness in his eyes as he released her hair from the confining cap. Beads of moisture glistened his skin in the over-bright light.

This close, she could see the fine lines radiating from the corners of his eyes, the tiny flecks of green in the grey. Clutching at straws, she breathed out deliberately into his face, taken aback when he smiled and shook his head.

'As any good chef knows, if you cut off the inner ends of the cloves before use there's little taint left on the breath. I was only teasing you earlier.'

'And Eloise?' she asked, fighting that part of her which wanted so badly to forget everything else. 'What were you doing with *her* earlier?'

The fingers he had slid around the back of her neck to caress the soft skin at her nape went still. Lips thinned, he said, 'She already told you. We went to Hudson.'

'You drove through *that* weather?'

'I've driven through worse.' He removed the hand holding her, expression suddenly remote. 'You're starting to sound like a wife.'

Kim was torn between two equally desperate needs. 'It's the part you gave me to play,' she got out. 'The part you're taking too much advantage of!'

There was a hint of cruelty in the curl of his lip. 'I've done nothing you haven't wanted too.'

'I know.' Her gaze was as direct as she could make it. 'And I'm not proud of it. But it still doesn't mean I'm willing to turn a blind eye while you indulge yourself at someone else's expense. If you'd married Eloise in the first place, none of this would have been necessary.'

'True,' he agreed. 'In which case, you and your brother would be facing prosecution right now.' He reached out and plucked one of the thick Turkish towels from the rail, thrusting it at her with a twisted little smile. 'You'll excuse me if I take a shower myself.'

'I'd have been better off with that than this!' she flung at him as he moved to step into the shower cubicle so recently vacated. 'And if you touch me again, I'll take the chance and leave!'

With the curtain half drawn, he stopped to look back at her standing there swathed now in the towel, an odd expression on his face. 'How would you propose to get back?'

'I'm not exactly a pauper,' she retorted. 'I have the means to buy a ticket home.'

There was a pause before he shrugged. 'Point taken.'

Kim stayed where she was for several seconds after the curtain was drawn and the water turned back on. She felt all churned up inside. He hadn't admitted making love to Eloise again, but he hadn't exactly denied it either. Not that it made any difference to her own situation whatever, providing he stuck to the implied agreement.

Seizing her nightdress from the chair where she had laid it ready, she went back to the bedroom. The towel she left in a heap at the door ready to be put into the basket in the morning. By the time Ryan came through, she was in bed, if still far from sleep.

He lay silently himself for some moments before easing over on to his side.

'Goodnight,' he said levelly.

Kim let out her breath on a faint sigh. So that was that. From now on the arrangement stayed purely businesslike.

Except that there was nothing businesslike about the ache deep inside her. And it wasn't, she knew, going to go away.

Lydia declined Ryan's suggestion that she accompany them into town. She had seen the office before, she said, and all her Christmas shopping was already done.

The journey was accomplished without any word of real note passing between them. Ryan himself seemed preoccupied, while Kim was too steeped in despondency to make the effort at conversation. How she was going to get through the coming festivities, she had no idea. If the pretence had seemed a mockery before, it was going to be doubly so at Christmas. Take presents, for instance. Husband and wife would obviously be expected to exchange them, and yet it would be such a hollow gesture. What on earth did one buy for a man who already had everything anyway?

The headquarters of the company were situated in Centre Town at Place de Canada. From the window of Mike's seventeenth-floor office, there was a magnificent view of the whole downtown area. Best seen at night, he said.

He took Kim on a tour of the various departments himself. There was little of the 'big boss around, must watch Ps and Qs' atmosphere to which she was accustomed. Most of the staff appeared to be on first-name terms.

The computer-room naturally occupied her interest the longest. She struck up an immediate rapport with the manager, leaving Mike, as he laughingly complained, totally out of his depth.

'We'd better go pick up that husband of yours,' he said in the end. 'We're meeting Eloise at one.'

'Did she never fancy coming into the business with you?' Kim asked lightly as they made their way towards the lifts.

'I'd have liked it,' he acknowledged, 'but she wasn't interested. She's made a big success of the boutique, so she isn't lacking in business sense. She's looking to open a second branch in the New Year.'

'Good for her.' Kim tried hard to sound warm and enthusiastic about it. 'You must be very proud of her.'

'Yes, I am,' he agreed. 'I just wish——' He broke off, smiling and shaking his head. 'I guess it'll happen some day.'

He was talking about marriage, Kim reflected. With no son of his own to take over when he went, he no doubt cherished the thought of a grandson. If Ryan had married Eloise, that happy event might even have been on its way. Not that she could see Ryan as a father—any more than she saw him as a husband. He didn't have what it took to make a success of either role.

They found him discussing theatre with Mike's secretary. Noting the sparkle in the girl's eyes, Kim wondered if that was *all* they had been discussing. The glance meeting hers as he came to his feet was devoid of mockery for once. She could almost have sworn that the smile he gave her held a genuine esteem.

'All through?' he asked.

'As far as it's possible to be in a couple of hours,' she returned lightly.

'There'll be other times,' said Mike. 'And plenty of them, I hope.' Perhaps fortunately, he wasn't looking directly at her. 'I invited my PA to lunch with us, by the way. He's meeting us in the lobby.'

The man who awaited them on the ground floor was in his late twenties. In looks and colouring, he reminded Kim a little of her brother, though minus the brashness. His name was Peter Leyton.

He and Ryan had not met before, as he had only been with the company around eight months. He was originally from Calgary, he told Kim on the way to the restaurant where they were to meet Eloise. She should take a trip out there, he said. Especially around Stampede time. She made the appropriate noises, avoiding Ryan's eyes. It was doubtful if she would ever see this country again outside travelogues on the television.

Eloise was late. They waited for her in the bar attached to the restaurant. She arrived looking very French and very chic in a trouser-suit of softest, pale green leather, treating all three men to a smile, but passing over Kim as if she weren't there.

At the table, she managed to seat herself between Ryan and Peter. Her mood was buoyant, her laughter infectious. Kim couldn't really blame either man for responding to her.

Peter, in particular, seemed mesmerised by her. Catching a certain look in Mike's eyes as he studied the young man at one point, Kim wondered if he could possibly have an ulterior motive in inviting him to lunch along with his daughter.

Suspicion became conviction before they finished the meal. It was Mike who drew the conversation around to the approaching vacation, asking Peter what his plans were.

'I can't say I have any special ones,' the latter confessed. 'My family's scattered all over the world. It must be five or six years since any of us managed to get together over Christmas.'

'Why not join our party up at St Justin?' suggested Mike on a casual note. 'The Lemoynes would fit you in somewhere.'

The younger man looked first startled, then suddenly heartened. 'Are you serious?' he asked.

'Sure I'm serious,' came the easy answer. 'Nobody should be on their own at Christmas. We're going up Thursday. You could make it Friday after close-down. We'd like to have you. Right?' The last to his daughter.

Her smile and shrug suggested indifference. 'The more the merrier.'

'That's settled, then. I'll ring Hélène this afternoon.'

'Thanks.' Peter looked as if he might be having a few doubts now that he really thought about it. 'It's good of you to take the trouble.'

'No trouble,' he was assured. 'You'll round up the numbers nicely.'

Looking at Eloise, Kim was pretty sure she couldn't care less about being the odd one out. Not when Ryan was going to be there. As to the latter himself, who could tell? His reasons for going to the Lodge at all were still open to interpretation.

The three of them spent the afternoon on Ste Catherine and Sherbrooke Streets. Kitted out with a one-piece ski-suit in scarlet and black, along with all the necessary accessories, Kim raised no objection when Ryan suggested they all split up for an hour to facilitate personal shopping.

Presents for the immediate family would be ostensibly from them both, and were his responsibility, but it still left her with the problem of what to buy for the man she was supposed to love and cherish.

Nothing too wildly expensive because she couldn't afford it, yet nothing too ordinary either.

She found what she was looking for in the shape of a tortoiseshell stud box inlaid with mother-of-pearl, and had it gift-wrapped right there in the shop. Catching sight of the sophisticated, fur-clad blonde through the mirrors backing the counter, she could hardly believe it was her own reflection she was looking at. Fine feathers not only made fine birds, she acknowledged ruefully, they created a whole new image. The sooner she got back to being plain Miss Anderson, the better.

The three of them had arranged to meet just inside the main entrance to one of the big department stores on Ste Catherine. Finding that the other two had already arrived was somehow no surprise. They were talking together with what appeared to be a fair degree of intimacy as Kim approached—an impression confirmed by the swift change of expression on Eloise's face when she looked up and saw her coming.

'Did you get everything you wanted?' she asked.

Did you? Kim wondered drily. 'I think so,' she said. Her eyes sought Ryan's, her emotions well under control. 'How about you?'

His smile was faint. 'There's time yet. I thought you might like to stay in town—maybe take in a show?'

Her glance went from his face to Eloise's, and back again. 'The three of us?'

'I have to get back to the shop,' claimed the other girl. 'You should come and take a look at my stock before you go home. I carry some very exclusive lines.'

'I'll see about getting you a cab,' said Ryan before Kim could answer. 'I'd wait here where it's warm, Cass,' he added. 'I shan't be long.'

He was gone more than ten minutes. She spent them looking at the huge display of tights and stockings in every shade and colour imaginable. One could match any outfit exactly here, she reckoned, although ice-blue legs might be carrying things a bit far in this winter climate.

On impulse, she bought a couple of pairs of sheer seven-denier black stockings with lacy garter tops. Nice to have to hand even if she didn't get round to wearing them here.

'Sorry it took so long,' Ryan apologised, coming up behind her as she paid the assistant. 'There was a line-up waiting for cabs. It's gone five. What say we find somewhere to have a nice quiet drink and wind down?'

The shoulders of his sheepskin coat were lightly flecked with beads of moisture. Melted snow, Kim surmised. She said slowly, 'Shouldn't we get straight back if the weather's taken a turn for the worse?'

'The forecast didn't indicate a heavy fall, but if the worst did come to the worst we could always spend the night at a hotel.' There was just a hint of irony. 'At the very least, you'd be assured of a bed to yourself.'

'Quite a bonus,' she agreed, borrowing his tone. 'I'll put my trust in the forecasters.'

He made no immediate effort to move, looking down at her with a curious expression on his face. Kim felt her chest go tight, the ache springing deep. If only things could have been different, came the thought. If only she could allow herself to care the way she wanted to care for this man. Totally without scruples he might be, but he still made her feel the way no one else had ever made her feel. Life simply wasn't fair!

'We're blocking the aisle,' she said thickly. 'Let's go and get that drink.'

With the car still parked back at the office car park, they took a cab to the same restaurant in the Old Quarter that they had used on the Friday. Only this time they were shown to a private room with a table set for two and its own well-stocked little bar.

'They do a particularly superb *fondue* here,' Ryan advised, pouring drinks for them both. 'We're early enough to enjoy it and still make the theatre before curtain-up. I hope you like Chekhov? I had quite a job getting tickets this late.'

'Why go to so much trouble?' Kim asked bluntly as he brought both glasses across to the table. 'We don't have to keep up the act when the family isn't around.'

Grey eyes held blue for a long, vibrant moment. 'Call it a peace-offering,' he said. 'I've behaved like a Philistine this last week. I'm not offering excuses. I'd just like to make it up to you a little, that's all.'

She gazed at him as a child gazed at a problem picture, the wind taken completely out of her sails. 'Why now?' she got out.

His mouth took on a slant. 'You made me see myself in a new light last night, and I didn't particularly care for what I saw. One thing I do want to make clear: there'd be no question of prosecution if you did decide to leave.'

'You mean you'd let me go?'

'If that was what you wanted. Naturally, I'd hope you'd stay and see it through with me.' He made a small, wry gesture. 'Telling my mother the truth now might not be advisable.'

'In other words, I still don't really have a choice, do I?' she said resignedly. 'I have to stay.'

'New ground rules,' he offered. 'I'll keep my hands off you.' His gaze dropped to her mouth, taking on a certain regret. 'Not that I'm going to pretend it will be easy.'

Flushing, she said, 'I'm as much to blame for what happened the other night as you are.'

The smile was brief. 'Hardly in the same sense. I'd every intention of having you, Kim, with or without your willing co-operation. I'm not sure what that makes me. Whatever it is, I'm not proud of it. As to Eloise...' he paused, shoulders lifting '...that was the biggest mistake of my life. The only thing I can say is that it wasn't premeditated.'

'She told me you were lovers,' Kim said softly. 'I gathered the impression it was going on for some time.'

There was a visible conflict mirrored in his eyes. When he answered it was with some obvious reticence. 'You gathered wrongly. It happened just the once.'

'The day you dried out at the Seguins'?' She kept her tone level. 'You're pleading entrapment, then?'

'I'm not *pleading* anything,' he denied. 'It happened, that's all there is to it.'

She searched the hard-boned features, not even sure what it was she was looking for. 'It's really none of my business, I suppose,' she said at length.

'I want it to be.' He reached across and took her hand, lifting it to his lips the way he had done once before, only this time without the mockery. His voice was soft, almost a caress in itself. 'You're a very special person, Kim. I took a mean advantage of a situation you were doing your best to rectify. All right, so perhaps I still think you were misguided to try covering up for your brother that way, but I appreciate your loyalty. I don't know any other woman who would take that kind of risk. I don't know any other woman who even comes close in terms of character, if it comes to that.'

Her heart was thudding against her ribcage, her whole attention riveted on the firm mouth. She could hardly get the words out. 'Thank you.'

'It's for me to thank *you*,' he insisted. 'You've given me a new insight. I'd like for us to go on seeing each other when we get back to London.' He quirked an eyebrow. 'Always providing you wanted it too, of course.'

She had to smile at that. He knew what he did to her; he knew she wouldn't say no. All the same...

'With what aim?' she heard herself asking, and saw something flicker deep down in the grey eyes.

'That,' he said, 'would remain to be seen, but I think we have what it takes to make a go of things.'

He could be talking about a serious relationship, or simply an ongoing affair, she realised; at the moment, the distinction wasn't the most important thing. She felt turned inside out by the sheer unexpectedness of it all. Ryan hadn't mentioned the word love, but he seemed to be hinting that he wasn't too far from it. As to her own feelings for him...

'I don't know what to say,' she managed huskily.

'Then don't say anything for now,' he advised. 'We'll talk about it again at the Lodge. Until then, let's just enjoy the companionship.'

# CHAPTER EIGHT

BARELY an hour's drive away from the city centre, the Laurentians region was another world. Snow-covered mountains were softened by numerous valleys containing the picturesque towns and villages. Kim was entranced by them all, especially Val-David with its Santa Claus village open eight months of the year.

Shortly after Ste-Agathe-des-monts, they left the highway and took to a minor road from which, judging by the banks to either hand, the latest snowfall had only recently been cleared. No pollution to diminish the gleaming whiteness out here.

'Another ten minutes,' promised Ryan, sensing the question before she could voice it. 'You'll see the lake from the top of the next rise.' He glanced sideways, smiling at her rapt expression. 'Glad you came?'

The two of them were alone in the Cadillac, the other three up ahead in the Lincoln. Eloise had shown little enthusiasm for the division, but her father had requested she take his place at the wheel. They would probably be at the Lodge already.

'I wouldn't have missed it,' she said, and knew it wasn't just the scenery she was thinking of. These next few days could well turn out to be the most important of her life.

The last three had certainly been the most confusing. For a man to change the way Ryan had changed was beyond anything she might have hoped

for. Oh, he was still the same dominant personality—
that was inborn in him—but his whole attitude
towards her was different. There had been no attempt
to further the physical side of their relationship; he
hadn't even kissed her. Whether he was waiting for
her to show some sign of wanting a renewal along
those lines, she had no idea. If she were honest with
herself, she had to admit to a certain yearning for the
overriding male ardour he had displayed before.

Some people, she thought wryly, were never
satisfied!

As he had said, the lake came into view as they
topped the rise. A wide band of ice carried red warning
flags some forty or fifty feet out. There were skaters
out there right now under the afternoon sun. Stretched
along the shore below them lay the little township of
St Justin, with the gantries of a ski-lift mounting the
slopes beyond.

The Lodge lay about half a mile outside the town
against a backdrop of tall Canadian pine. Built almost
entirely of wood, it looked like an overgrown, three-
storeyed log cabin slung between two huge stone
chimney stacks. All the rooms facing to the front had
covered verandas running along outside. Lovely to sit
out on in the summer, Kim reflected, though hardly
in use at this time of the year.

There was a layer of hard-packed snow over the car
park. Ryan dropped both her and the luggage off at
the main doors of the place before driving in to find
a space among the dozen or so other vehicles already
parked. She could see the Lincoln from where she
stood, but she made no move to go indoors and find

the rest of the party. She wanted Ryan with her when she faced Eloise.

He came up the steps with lithe assurance, tall and powerful in the thick mackinaw and white roll-necked sweater. 'Cases too heavy for you?' he grinned, hefting them up. 'So much for equality!'

'There's more to it than mere brute strength,' she responded, matching his mood. 'A matter of brain power.'

The smile was in his eyes, devastating in impact. 'Where yours is concerned, I might even concede a point or two. At least open the door for me.'

She did, preceding him inside to hold it open until he was through. The big open lobby had a roaring fire in the wide stone fireplace at one end, its boarded floor sanded and polished to a lovely golden glow and scattered with hand-pegged rugs. A huge and beautifully decorated tree stood in the right-angle created by the staircase. The warmth of central heating drove any lingering chill from hands and feet.

There were several other people in the room. The middle-aged woman writing in a ledger behind the long desk at the rear looked up smilingly as they approached.

'So good to see you again, Ryan!' she exclaimed. 'It's been a long time!'

'Hasn't it, though?' His tone was easy. 'I'd like you to meet my wife. Cass, this is Hélène Lemoyne.'

Kim put out a reluctant hand. She had almost forgotten the necessity to keep up the pretence. 'Hello.'

'You're more than welcome.' The other's English was accented, her tone warm. 'Mike said to tell you they would see you down here for drinks before dinner.'

Ryan laughed. 'Stealing a crafty nap, eh? Which room did you give us?'

'Seven, on the second floor. Can you manage your bags, or shall I call one of the boys?'

'I'll cope.' He was already swinging both suitcases up again. 'Take the key, darling.'

He had used the endearment so naturally, Kim thought, feeling the warm little glow in her chest as she moved in the direction of the staircase leading to the upper regions. None of that underlying and hateful sardonic manner she had come so much to dread. Had things gone as originally planned, they would have been on their way back to England tonight. For the first time, she allowed herself to be wholeheartedly glad that they were still here.

Tony had received the news that she wouldn't be back for Christmas with ill-concealed elation. Whatever he was planning, she didn't want to know. As she had telephoned direct, he had naturally assumed she was ringing from Devon. If Ryan was serious about continuing the relationship when they got back, she might have to tell her brother the truth—or at least part of it—but she would concern herself with that if and when it became necessary. She was counting on nothing until it became fact.

'It's right on there,' Ryan urged at the head of the initial flight of stairs as she made to start up to the next floor. 'They count ground as first over here.' He fell into step at her side, a suitcase swinging easily from each hand. 'It's barely three. Once we've unloaded these we could take a walk down into town, if you like?'

'That would be great,' she said, and stifled the tiny pang of disappointment. Genuinely married couples might well spend the afternoon making love, but was it really what she wanted under present circumstances? Ryan was behaving impeccably; she could do no less than appreciate his efforts to make up for what had gone before.

The room they had been allocated was light and airy, with a superb view out over the lake to the snow-capped range. There was an adjoining and well-equipped bathroom too. No double bed, Kim observed, but a pair of queen-sized instead. Enough room to share, came the thought unbidden.

Already dressed for outdoors, she only needed the addition of a knitted woollen hat pulled down well over her ears to complete the outfit. Ryan left his own head bare. Telling him that more than seventy per cent of body heat was lost through the head smacked too much of wifely concern, she figured, and kept her mouth shut.

There was no sign of Eloise when they went downstairs, much to her relief. Once Peter arrived, they would become a foursome whether Eloise liked it or not. Mike was barking up the wrong tree if he had an eye on his PA as a potential son-in-law, though; Kim was pretty sure of that. Peter's was too gentle a personality to prevail over Ryan's attraction.

The air outside was still and crisp. Hands snug in sheepskin gloves, boots crunching over frosted snow, they swung side by side down the narrow footpath which came out on the town outskirts. Occasionally,

Ryan put out a hand to stop her from falling on a particularly slippery patch, but for the most part there was space between them. Kim wanted him close—wanted his arm about her shoulders the way another couple they passed were walking. They still had to achieve that kind of companionship.

'Has it changed much since you were last up here?' she asked as they joined the road running alongside the lake.

'Quite a lot,' he said. 'The ski school brought in a lot of new blood.' He slanted a glance at her. 'How good are you on the slopes?'

'Fair,' was all she would allow herself.

'We'll see in the morning, once we've got you kitted out.'

Just the two of them? she wondered, but refrained from voicing the question. If she was going to learn to trust Ryan at all, Eloise had to be a part of that trust.

The town boasted several cafés, a couple of good restaurants, and a solitary cinema. The people who came to St Justin were here for the peace and quiet as much as the excellent skiing, Kim surmised. Things would probably liven up in the evenings when the *après-ski* enthusiasts took over. There were always those for whom the day wasn't complete without the ritual letting-down of hair over a drink or two or three.

They had coffee at one of the cafés overlooking the lake, and watched the few skaters still left on the ice. Sunset was less than an hour away, with full dark right on its heels. There was more snow forecast overnight, and ideal conditions for tomorrow. Kim hoped she was going to be good enough to keep pace with Ryan.

It was nine or ten months since she had last done any serious skiing.

'Glad you decided to stay?' he asked on a humorous note during a lull in conversation, and she found herself smiling back.

'I can think of worse places to be.'

'And worse people to be with?' He laughed and shook his head. 'Don't answer that.'

'It hasn't all been bad,' she admitted, dropping her gaze a little.

'No, indeed.' His tone had softened. 'In fact, parts of it have been unforgettable. Don't shy away from it,' he added as her head jerked. 'There's nothing wrong in two people vitally attracted to each other wanting to make love. It's the most natural thing in the world.'

'I hardly know you,' she murmured.

'A matter I'm doing my best to rectify. If there's anything you especially want to know, you only have to ask.'

Temptation came and went. He was talking about background, not private and personal emotions. Whatever he'd done with Eloise, he hadn't been prepared to make any lasting commitment to her. She had to be satisfied with that.

'If I think of anything, I will,' she promised lightly. 'Shouldn't we be starting back? It's going to be dark by the time we get there.'

'My night vision is pretty good,' he responded, equally lightly, but he was getting to his feet. 'You're right, we still have to unpack and change for dinner. We eat early up here, by the way. Most folk are ready for bed by midnight after a day on the slopes. Not mandatory, of course—especially as we didn't get started yet. We can always drive back in to town later if you feel like it.'

'Let's play it by ear,' Kim suggested, not sure what she was going to feel like later.

'Fine by me,' he agreed.

The last of the skaters were coming up from the lake as they emerged from the café. The sight of Eloise in an outfit of emerald-green was somehow no surprise. She was with a small group of people around her own age, and was laughing over some shared joke until her eyes fell on Ryan. She said something to the man at her side, who paused to wait for her, then came on over, avoiding any contact with Kim's gaze.

'You should have joined us,' she said. 'The boots can be hired.'

'It's been too long since I skated,' returned Ryan easily. 'I'll stick to the slopes this time.'

Dark eyes acquired a sudden spark. 'Then I challenge you to a race down the Black run in the morning! Not for the novice, I'm afraid,' she added to Kim, still without turning her head more than a fraction towards her.

'Oh, I think I could manage to get down in one piece,' the latter came back recklessly, not about to let herself be left on any sidelines.

This time Eloise did look at her, and not with pleasure. 'If you wish,' said her voice; if you insist, said her tone. 'The lift opens at nine. If we're there early enough we can cut the first tracks.'

'Always providing it's stopped snowing by then.' Ryan sounded amenable enough. 'Are you staying down here for the evening?'

'Of course. There's a disco at Jacques'. Why don't you come?'

'Not my scene,' he said. 'We'll see you at the ski lift, then.'

Kim couldn't withstand a faintly malicious pleasure as the other turned abruptly to go back to her waiting friend. Ryan could hardly have made the message clearer.

'Sorry for not consulting you,' he proffered, 'but that kind of frenetic activity leaves me cold.'

'Me too.' She was speaking the truth, although at that moment she would have claimed an equal dislike of anything in order to be in accord with him.

His voice was very soft, creating a delicious little tingle along her spine. 'You're a woman after my own heart!'

That was true too, she acknowledged, falling into step beside him. Only not just his heart; she wanted all of him. She had read of love as a blinding force, but the way she felt about this man surpassed even her wildest imaginings. It was like having a volcano ready to explode inside her!

Darkness had descended before they reached the Lodge. The whole front elevation was strung with fairy-lights, the centrepiece an illuminated cross that had to be visible for miles. Christmas starts right here, thought Kim as they mounted the steps. Beyond that, she didn't want to contemplate as yet.

Inside was warmth and colour and sound, as the dozen or more people sitting or standing in groups around the lobby vied with each other in cheerful conversation. Mike lifted an arm to wave them over to one such group, and introduced Kim to the two middle-aged couples.

Neither of the women spoke any English at all, and were appreciative of her efforts to make herself understood in French.

'Lydia despaired of ever becoming a grandmama,' declared one a little archly. 'You must hurry to satisfy her.'

'We'll do our best,' responded Ryan on a light note, avoiding his mother's eye. 'Excuse us, won't you? We still have to change for dinner.'

The coveted arm came about Kim's shoulders to turn her back in the direction of the stairs, remaining there until they reached the foot. She felt bereft when he removed it, although he remained close enough at her side on the ascent to the upper floor.

Her heartbeats quickened again as they approached their room. It needed another hour until dinner. Time enough for anything he might have in mind. Making love with this new and different Ryan was an experience she craved.

There was no lamp lit in the room. Kim switched one on, and went over to the window to draw the curtains. The lights of the town twinkled and shimmered against the silvered whiteness of the mountainside at its back. Even as she watched, the first gentle flakes began to fall.

'It's snowing,' she said, unnecessarily because Ryan was standing right behind her. 'How will Eloise get back if it comes down very thick?'

'That,' he said, 'is her problem.' He pulled the cord to close the curtains, then turned her towards him, sliding his hands under her hair to cup her face and tilt it upwards. With his back to the solitary dim light, it was difficult to read his expression, but there was no doubting the tenderness in his touch. 'I'm about to break those new ground rules,' he added. 'Do you object?'

'Will it make any difference if I say yes?' she asked huskily.

The laugh came low. 'Not one iota!'

'Then I won't waste my breath.'

She had none to waste anyway as he found her mouth. She returned the kiss with mounting passion, body trembling to the feel of his hands.

Her jacket had already been discarded downstairs. He peeled the polo-necked sweater from her with dexterity and dropped it on the floor, following it seconds later with her brassière. His fingers felt cold at first to her skin, but they soon warmed up. Kim closed her eyes to the exquisite sensations he elicited in his exploration of her tingling, tautly peaking flesh. There was only one man who could do this to her; one man who had ever managed to invade that deep-down part of her never before acknowledged.

Her lips moved with slow sensuality against his, harshening his breath and drawing immediate response. Without breaking off the kiss, he slid an arm beneath her knees and swung her up to carry her across to the nearest of the two beds. She helped him remove the rest of her clothing, lying there watching through slitted eyes while he stripped himself, the restless yearning sending tremors through every part of her body.

The grey eyes were on fire when he came back to her, but he didn't rush things. His mouth was almost gentle at first, acquiring passion by slow degrees in tune with her arousal—moving down to the vulnerable hollow of her throat and on to the soft swell of her breasts with a lingering attention that drove her wild with desire, his tongue a flickering, tormenting flame she had no wish to put out.

Shafts of pleasure exploded deep inside to draw guttural little moans from her lips. She clutched at him as he moved on down the length of her body, eyes half closed in an ecstasy of sensation, every nerve pulsatingly alive. She wanted to scream, to shout, to let go of all inhibition in a hedonistic orgy.

The feel of him inside her was incredible. He made it last, building the pace very slowly, very gradually until they could neither of them hold out a single moment longer. Like going into free-fall, came the final fleeting thought.

They must have fallen asleep in each other's arms for a few minutes. When Kim opened her eyes again she could feel the cramp in her shoulder where the dark head rested. Ryan came awake the moment she moved, easing his weight from her by shifting on to his side, but taking her with him so that they lay face to face. She could feel his breath on her cheek, see the deep luminous glow in his eyes. The embers stirred into new life.

'What time is it?' she whispered.

'I don't know,' he admitted. 'Right now, I don't much care.' His lips sought the fluttering pulse at her temple, light as the brush of a bird's wing. 'I'd rather stay here and make love to you again.'

'We can't,' she murmured, stifling the impulse. 'They're expecting us down to dinner.'

His laugh was low. 'Meaning it would embarrass you to have them suspect what might have kept us?'

She tried to keep her tone light. 'Something like that.'

He was silent for a moment, studying her. This close, there was no turning away from the penetrating gaze. When he spoke again it was on a neutral note. 'Would you still feel the same if we were really married?'

Kim swallowed on the sudden dryness in her throat. 'Probably.'

'Little prude.' He sounded amused again, though not in any hurtful fashion. 'They've all done the same thing we've just done—even my mother and Mike.' He pressed another swift kiss to her temple, and rolled away from her to sit upright on the edge of the bed. 'There's always tonight.'

And tomorrow, she thought, controlling the urge to call him back. Christmas Eve. A time for all kinds of miracles to happen. All she asked for was the one.

Dinner was a highly communal and casual affair, with no table seating less than eight. Kim found herself doing full justice to a four-course meal any restaurant would have been proud to serve.

Yves did all the cooking himself, Lydia informed her. He had trained in Paris and spent several years at one of Montreal's top hotels before meeting Hélène and deciding to branch out into something new and different. A small and wiry man with a retiring, almost diffident nature, he put in a brief appearance after the meal to receive the accolades due to him.

They played charades for the first hour or so. Never a particular lover of organised games before, Kim en-

tered into the spirit of things with a will when Ryan
showed sportsmanship himself. Later, there was
dancing to taped music in a cleared area of the vast
lounge. None of the modern upbeat stuff they would
be doing down at the town disco, but with enough
Latin American numbers to keep the atmosphere
lively.

'It's been ages since I last attempted a cha-cha-cha!'
Kim admitted laughingly, sinking back into her seat
after one hectic round. 'I think I dislocated a hip!'

'It looked good from here,' declared Mike. 'The
two of you could take up competition work with a
little more practice.'

'She's a great little mover,' agreed Ryan with an
intonation that brought swift colour to her cheeks.
'We'll have to see about the practice.' He caught his
stepfather's glance towards the wall clock nearby, and
added levelly, 'Eloise will be OK, Mike. She's with
friends.'

'She isn't going to make it back up here tonight if
she leaves it much longer,' he growled. 'The snow isn't
due to peter out until the early hours.'

'In which case, she'll simply have to stay over
somewhere until morning,' said his wife on a prac-
tical note, drawing a rare frown.

'It's unlikely there'll be a room going spare anywhere in town this time of year.'

'I'll go and find her while the going's still good, if
you like?' offered Ryan without expression, and his
stepfather's face lightened.

'I'd be grateful. That crowd she's with is a bit too
off-beat for my taste.'

Kim said nothing. The smile on her lips was purely for effect. Ryan had jumped into the breach a shade too quickly for comfort—although she supposed he had been left with little real choice considering Mike's obvious concern. Parents worried about their offspring, no matter what age they were; that she could appreciate. But Eloise was more than capable of taking care of her own interests.

She kept the smile fixed as Ryan went from the room. Surprisingly, it was Lydia who expressed disapprobation.

'The girl is twenty-six, Mike. She isn't going to thank you for putting her in this position.'

Had he dispatched anyone else to fetch her home, that might have been true, thought Kim sardonically. Ryan was another matter altogether. With the weather the way it was, there was even a chance neither of them might make it back before morning. In fact, she wouldn't put it past the two of them to have engineered the whole thing this way!

Be rational, she told herself severely at that point. If Ryan had wanted Eloise he could have had her on a full-time basis this past year. She had to put her faith in the way he had been with her earlier—the emotion they had shared so devastatingly. Jealousy was soul-destroying, especially when it had no real basis.

He had left at ten. By eleven-thirty the party was beginning to disperse, the revelry to wind down. The appearance of the missing pair just on the midnight hour brought a mingling of emotions in which relief played only a part.

Eloise looked sparkling, the glance she directed at Kim holding an unmistakable light of triumph.

'We waited for the blowers,' she said for the benefit of all. 'Ryan had a job getting through. The snow stopped a few minutes ago, by the way, so we should be OK for tomorrow.'

'It's tomorrow now.' Mike was heaving himself to his feet. 'I guess I'm for bed.'

'Me too,' said Lydia. She looked tired, with lines about eyes and mouth that Kim had never noted before. 'The three of you will probably be gone before we get down,' she added. 'I hope you're not planning on skiing off-*piste*. You know how treacherous new snow on top of ice can be.'

'Don't worry about it,' her son assured her. 'We'll see you at lunch.'

He watched his mother cross the room, the look of concern in his eyes replaced by some other, less definable emotion as he brought his attention back to the table and the two still seated there.

'Time we were all thinking of retiring if we're going to be fit and fresh for morning,' he said. 'We'll need to be away by eight-thirty, so it's breakfast no later than eight. I already told Hélène.'

'One drink,' Eloise appealed. She held his gaze provocatively. 'After all, I had to abandon my last one.'

Kim got to her feet. 'Count me out,' she said without undue emphasis. 'I'm going up. Goodnight, Eloise.'

The other scarcely bothered to turn her head. 'Goodnight.'

Ryan couldn't very well leave her sitting there alone, Kim reasoned as she climbed the stairs, although she had hoped he might do just that. One drink wasn't going to take very long, and they had the rest of the night in front of them. She could wait. What she couldn't do was stomach any more of Eloise's self-satisfaction at present.

## CHAPTER NINE

Kim looked down between her dangling, ski-shod feet to the white slope sparkling in the sunlight. Other than a slight whirring sound from the cable, the silence was absolute. The temperature was still below zero, the branches of the pines rimming the trail weighted down with snow. Some small animal had ventured halfway across the open area before losing courage and heading back to the safety of the trees, leaving a double track of footprints in mute testimony.

Occupying the chair at her side, Eloise had her attention firmly fixed on the trackless slopes above. Ryan had insisted the two of them share, and had himself taken the second chair in line. He was several feet below them at the moment, though hardly out of mind.

It had been gone one when he finally came to bed. Kim had feigned sleep, and he had made no attempt to waken her. The failure of the alarm to go off this morning had left little time for anything in the rush to make breakfast for eight, although what she would have said to him in any case, she wasn't at all sure. She had no legitimate claim on him.

There was no alpine cafeteria at the top of the lift, just a shed containing the gear to return the chairs downhill again. One man stood on duty. He waved a hand to them as they skied down the slight gradient out of range of the next chair in line.

Ryan joined them a moment later. He looked, Kim thought, so professional in the tight black pants and padded jacket, with the white of his sweater showing above the neckline as the only relief. Her scarlet went well with the colour scheme—but then so did Eloise's turquoise.

The latter was already turning to ski off on a traverse across the flat, bare expanse. Sticks ready for the push, Ryan gave Kim an appraising glance.

'From what I remember of the Black, it's going to be fast and furious. Are you sure you're up to it?'

'I'll be fine,' she said with determination. 'I might not be in the race, but I'll get down OK.'

His smile gave her reason to believe her fears might, after all, be misplaced. 'Good enough.'

Standing at the top of the run they were to ski some minutes later, she felt that confidence ebb a little. Fast and furious, he had said. What he hadn't said was 'near vertical' in the first few hundred feet. The only way she was going to make it down there without breaking her neck in the process was by a tight and regular series of turns to slow her speed, and even then with every chance of wrapping herself round a tree at that first bend.

Nothing of which trepidation she allowed to show on her face. She wouldn't give Eloise the satisfaction she was so obviously looking for. 'I'll bring up the rear,' she offered. 'That way I'll be sure of the track without having to keep an eye on the markers.'

Ryan hesitated just a moment before nodding agreement. 'Just take it easy,' he advised.

Eloise pushed off first, with Ryan a bare second behind. They were going to schuss the whole slope,

Kim realised in a mixture of horror and admiration as she watched the speed build. Considering the angle where the marked run curved in among the trees, there was going to be little margin for error.

She let out pent-up breath on a little sigh when first one and then the other braked the wild flight with a couple of well-controlled turns before reaching the bend. Then they were gone, and it was time for her to put her money where her mouth was and follow in their wake.

Over-cautious at first, she had relaxed sufficiently by the time she reached the bend to start enjoying the experience. From there, the trail wound down through the trees in a series of narrow curves which presented problems of a different kind, but she negotiated them without mishap, pausing for a breather where the trail emerged into the open again.

She could see the other two some quarter of a mile or so ahead and below. They had paused on the brow of another steep fall-away, the colours of their suits needle-sharp against the skyline. Even as she watched, the two figures merged together in a manner that drove a dagger-thrust deep into her chest.

The embrace lasted mere seconds, but it was enough. Jaw clenched, she watched them break apart, heard the distant sound of Eloise's laughter carried on the crisp, still air.

Then Ryan was turning, looking back up to the trees and lifting an arm in acknowledgement when he spotted her, and she was waving back like an auto- maton. So much for all the stupid, naïve hopes of the last couple of days. He hadn't changed. He had simply been playing her along—the same way he was playing

Eloise along. His only interest was in satisfying his own animal lusts!

Fury swamped the immediate hurt. He was going to pay for this! If it was the last thing she did, he was going to pay! I'll tell them all the truth, she thought savagely. I'll stand up in the middle of lunch today and tell them who I really am and why I'm here!

For a moment or two that notion held sway before numb acceptance took its place. She couldn't do it. Not to someone in Lydia's condition.

Standing here like this, she could feel the cold beginning to strike through. She moved out into the sunlight, stooping to adjust the ski fastenings with fingers made clumsy by the trembling she couldn't control. To have fallen this far for any man in little more than a week was bad enough; coupled with the way he had forced her into the situation in the first place, it was close to insanity! Only not any more. From this moment on, they were enemies again.

She was sufficiently in control of herself by the time she completed the run to accept Ryan's acclaim with an outer nonchalance. Eloise made no effort to disguise her impatience.

'We were about to come looking for you,' she claimed. 'We thought you'd taken a fall. We're going back up to do the Red,' she added without waiting for any reply.

Resting on her sticks, Kim avoided direct confrontation with the grey gaze, afraid of giving too much away. 'I'll settle for a hot drink in the café,' she said, 'and wait for you.'

'We'll all have a drink,' said Ryan, jerking her head as if it had been pulled by a string.

'No!' Seeing the line appear between dark brows, she tried to soften the harsh refusal. 'I don't want to spoil things for everybody just because I'm a bit out of practice. If I overdo it now, I'll be too tired to enjoy the rest of the day.'

As an excuse it held little water, and she knew it, but it was the best she could come up with. Ryan studied her thoughtfully for a moment before lifting his shoulders in a brief shrug.

'You know your own limitations. We shouldn't be more than half an hour.'

Eloise looked like a cat with a bowl of cream as the two of them moved off towards the lift. Reaching the building housing the café and shop, Kim turned in her skis before going through to the cheerfully decorated servery.

The blast of heat from the blowers brought life back to her chilled extremities, but did little to ease her frigidity of mind. From where she sat with her coffee, she could see the line of people waiting to board the chair-lift. Ryan and Eloise were just about to go, poised to allow the double chair to come beneath them. Then they were up and away, heads close together in obvious and mutually desirous communion.

Taxing him with duplicity would be a waste of time; he was hardly going to admit it. What she had to do was turn the tables on him somehow. The question was what on earth one did to hurt a man so totally devoid of sensitivity.

She was no nearer a solution when the pair finally returned some forty minutes later. Smug was the only word to apply to Eloise.

'Too many amateurs up there now,' she declared. 'Only the experienced should be allowed to ski the upper slopes.'

'Wouldn't that be a bit of a catch twenty-two?' suggested Kim, weathering the patronising glance turned her way. 'One needs the experience to gain the experience. After all, there had to be a first time for you too.'

'I've been skiing since I was five years old,' the other replied loftily, either missing the point of the argument or deliberately ignoring it—Kim wasn't sure which.

'Coffee?' asked Ryan into the pause. He sounded faintly amused.

Eloise shook her head. 'I'll wait until we get back to the Lodge.'

They went back the way they had come, in the Cadillac, the snow tyres gripping the icy road without difficulty. Lydia and Mike had just returned from a stroll into town.

'There's dog-sled racing this afternoon across at Val-Damase,' Mike announced over coffee in the lounge. 'Anybody interested?'

'We're going skiing again,' claimed his daughter. Her eyes sought Ryan's, her smile intimate. 'I have to equal this morning's score.'

Kim said swiftly, 'If you're planning on going yourselves, I'd love to see the sled racing.'

Ryan gave her a sharp glance. 'In that case, we'll all go.'

'Not me.' Eloise was tight-lipped. '*I'm* going skiing.'

'On your own?' Her father looked concerned. 'There's an avalanche warning out.'

'Let's make the return match tomorrow,' suggested Ryan. 'There probably won't be too many up there Christmas morning.'

She herself was one who wouldn't be, for certain, thought Kim, watching Eloise's expression undergo a subtle alteration as she held Ryan's gaze. Let the two of them enjoy each other's company free of restriction. Her own part in this farce was to all intents and purposes over. If it weren't for Lydia, she would already be on her way home.

'I'm going up to change for lunch,' she said, unable to sit there a moment longer and keep her feelings hidden. 'See you all later.'

Ryan followed her up to the room almost at once. Closing the door, he said levelly, 'What's wrong?'

She kept her head averted as she took clean underwear from a drawer. Prevarication was useless when he was so obviously aware of her mood.

'Everything,' she responded flatly. 'I was an idiot to let myself be conned into believing in you even for a minute. Leopards don't change their spots.'

'True,' he agreed. 'But then, I'm no leopard.' The pause was brief but weighted. 'So what changed your mind again?'

'I saw you,' she said. 'Kissing Eloise on the mountain. Not that I think she can count on any sincerity either.' She straightened, still without turning her head towards him. 'Your trouble is, you want it all, Ryan. Anything and everything you can get away with! *My* trouble is I'm too gullible. I let things happen without studying the outcome. I'll see this particular mistake out because I won't be held responsible for what might happen to your mother if she knew you for the liar and cheat you really are, but it won't be on the same terms.'

The pause after she finished speaking was lengthy. She had almost reached the conclusion he wasn't going to answer at all when he said expressionlessly, 'Is that it?'

She turned then, viewing the hard, incisive lines of his face with a tensing of muscle and sinew. 'Isn't it enough?'

'Not quite, no.' He still hadn't altered his tone. 'Are you always so quick to jump to conclusions?'

'Meaning you were only taking something out of Eloise's eye this morning?' Her sarcasm was biting. 'And I suppose you spent that hour last night in idle chit-chat!'

There was a hint of cruelty in the slow curl of his lip. 'Not exactly idle.'

'I'm sure!' The anger that had carried her this far was fast giving way to pain. It was in an effort to bolster it that she tagged on scathingly, 'Any time, any place—that just about sums you up! Only don't expect to apply it to *me* any more. I lost interest.'

'Sure you did.' His voice mocked her. 'You know, I really thought you were different, Kim. Turns out you're just like all the rest—blind to everything outside your own narrow little viewpoint. And if I'm not prepared to accept that loss of interest, what then?'

She stared at him, breast rising and falling in agitation. 'You have to!'

'I don't *have* to do anything,' he stated. 'Lunch won't be for another half-hour. Supposing you prove to me just how uninterested you are?'

Kim backed away as he moved towards her, until the feel of the bed-edge at the back of her knees stopped her in her tracks. There was no give in his expression, no sign of the man she had known these last few days. As an act, it had been without equal; she had been totally fooled. This reversion to type was all the more distressing for that contrast.

'I don't want you,' she whispered desperately. 'Can't you get that through your head? It's all been a big mistake.'

'That I can go along with,' he came back grimly. 'And, having made it already, we may as well compound it.'

He was still wearing the snugly fitting ski-pants and white sweater, the jacket having been left downstairs in the lobby along with her own. He took off both the sweater and the woollen shirt beneath at the same time, tossing them aside and following them with his boots. Kim watched numbly as he inserted both thumbs under the elaschticated waistband and slid the pants down over lean hips.

'Join me,' he invited sardonically, sitting down on the bed to extract his legs from the narrow stems. 'Unless you'd rather I did the undressing for you?'

She said it through clenched teeth. 'I'll see you in hell first!'

He grabbed her wrist as she started to move, yanking her down on to the bed and rolling to cover her. The glitter in his eyes wasn't all anger; there was passion of a different nature there too. His mouth lacked any hint of gentleness, bruising the soft inner flesh as he forced her lips apart.

The thrust of his tongue was a violation in itself. She brought her teeth together with viciousness and tasted blood before he jerked away.

'That,' he gritted, 'is going to cost you!'

He stripped her with a single-mindedness of purpose which left little room for resistance, although she tried hard enough. His weight pinioned her, dragging a frantic little cry from her lips as she felt the potent demand. Then he was kissing her again, only this time there was no drawing back, no letting up at all until she finally began to respond against every instinct. Only then did he take full possession of her trembling, weak-kneed body, merciless in his driving, overwhelming force.

There was no lingering aftermath this time. Kim forced herself upright as the bathroom door slammed behind him. She felt mentally as well as bodily debased. No man, she thought painfully, had the right to do what Ryan had just done. He was the one in the wrong, not her.

She was wearing a wrap and sitting with her back to the door when he emerged again. She listened without moving to the sounds he made as he dressed.

'Hadn't you better get ready?' he asked when the silence had grown to unbearable proportions. His tone was cool and controlled. 'We'll be sitting down to lunch in less than ten minutes.'

Had so little time really passed since his last such pronouncement? Kim wondered numbly. She seemed to have been sitting here like this for hours.

'I'm not hungry,' she said, and wondered again at the steadiness of her voice. 'You'll have to go down without me.'

'No.' It was an unequivocal denial. 'We'll go down together, and act the way we're expected to act.'

'Why should I care about the way things might look?' she demanded, losing the unnatural calm in sudden searing rage. 'Why should I give a damn about any of it?'

'Because both your brother's future and your own still rests with me,' he came back hardily. 'There's time yet for an attack of conscience on my part regarding the cover-up.'

'That's a word you've no concept of!' She was on her feet and facing him, the anger too intense for caution to hold any sway. 'You don't care about your mother. All you care about is saving face!'

Dressed now in trousers and casual shirt, he looked back at her with dangerously narrowed eyes. 'And, having established that much, you'd do well to remember it. You've got five minutes to put some clothes on.'

Briefly, she considered defying him. Was there anything he could do to her that he hadn't done already?

Plenty, came the answer; there was nothing she would put past him.

Biting her lip, she took up the garments he had removed previously, and moved towards the bathroom, passing him with head held high.

'I'll do it for your mother's sake,' she said contemptuously, 'not yours.'

Ryan made no answer. His face was a granite mask. If there had been any truth at all in the regard he had professed to be developing for her, it was gone for good now. Well, that cut both ways. She had never hated anyone the way she hated him.

Her performance at lunch was the best she could manage under the circumstances. That it wasn't quite good enough was evidenced by the increasingly sharp glances Lydia kept directing at the two of them. The woman was no fool; she could sense the discord. In all probability, she would put it down to a simple marital tiff, Kim reassured herself.

Eloise had reversed her decision to ski alone. The races were worth watching, she conceded when Mike brought the subject up, and there was always tomorrow.

'It might be an idea if you wait till the afternoon,' said her father casually. 'I thought the six of us could attend the service down at the church.'

Until that moment, Kim had completely forgotten that Peter Leyton would be joining them later. From the look on her face, so had Eloise. The more the merrier, she had said so blandly when the invitation had been extended; hardly the sentiment she was expressing now.

It was Ryan who settled the matter, tone unrevealing. 'A gesture in the right direction. We'll ski after lunch.'

'On top of the kind of meal Yves will be serving?' Eloise sounded anything but enthusiastic. 'The lift may not even be working in the afternoon!'

'In which case, we'll make it Boxing Day instead,' he returned. 'What time do you expect Peter up here?'

'Not before six,' replied Mike. 'We'll be back by then. He's an excellent skier himself, by the way.'

He was flogging a dead horse, thought Kim. Where his daughter was concerned, no other man but Ryan

would do. How many times had it been said that love
was blind?

Sitting there across from her now, he could still
tauten her stomach muscles with his dark attraction;
that was something over which she unfortunately had
no control. It was difficult even now to credit the
depths to which he'd stoop. Whichever way one looked
at what had happened between them earlier, it came
out close to rape. Anger because she had dared accuse
him of double-dealing was no excuse.

She was getting herself all worked up again, she
acknowledged ruefully, and to no purpose. From now
on, she had to stay aloof.

Dog-sled racing was fast, exciting, and dangerous to
both participant and spectator at times. Kim found
herself caught up in the general atmosphere to a point
where she could almost forget her immediate
problems.

It took Lydia to bring her down to earth again in
a lull between races when Ryan and Mike had gone
to fetch mugs of the hot coffee on sale from a kiosk,
and Eloise was talking with some acquaintances.

'I realise you're probably going to think me the
worst kind of interfering mother-in-law,' she said, 'but
Christmas is no time for disagreements—especially
when it's your first together.'

Kim couldn't bring herself to look the older woman
straight in the eye. Denying the absence of friction
between her and Ryan would be pointless when it was
so obviously apparent.

'Just a difference of opinion,' she murmured. 'It
will blow over.'

'Not if it's about what I think it's about.' Lydia was not to be fobbed off. 'You mustn't be jealous of Eloise. They've known each other a long time, but you're the one Ryan chose as his wife.' There was a pause, a change of tone. 'I can't pretend to have been anything but devastated when he presented us with the news, but that's behind us now. I'm only glad I was wrong in thinking you an opportunist.'

Kim's smile felt stiff. 'What makes you so sure I'm not?'

'You're just not the type, my dear.' The other's tone had softened again. 'One only has to watch you watching him to see how much you love him.'

Hardly the first to mistake lust for love, came the cynical thought; she had done it herself, hadn't she?

'It makes the world go round,' she said with creditable lightness. She indicated a new team of huskies being harnessed ready for the next race. 'If noise is anything to go by, they should be outright winners!'

Lydia accepted the change of subject without demur, but her expression was still a little troubled. Should the atmosphere between her son and his 'wife' not improve, that concern may have undesired effects, Kim acknowledged with resignation. In public, at least, she had to make some effort towards an apparent reconciliation, no matter what it took.

The two men were returning with the coffee. She forced herself to meet the grey eyes as she took a steaming mug from Ryan, to smile and murmur her thanks. His expression was difficult to define, though his response was easy enough. Lydia gave her an approving nod.

They saw two more races before calling it a day. Darkness had fallen by the time they got back to the Lodge, and the lamps were already lit. Peter had arrived about an hour ago, Hélène advised.

'I still don't see why you had to invite him,' said Eloise as they all made their way upstairs. 'He's going to feel a complete outsider.'

'Only if we let him,' returned her father. 'I expect you to treat him like one of the family while we're here.'

Her expression was wooden. 'I shan't do anything to upset him.'

She wouldn't be doing much to make him feel at home either, Kim surmised. So it would be up to the rest of them. Not that she herself belonged in any real sense, but he wasn't to know that.

Alone again in the bedroom with Ryan, she made a show of sorting out something to wear for the evening. She could feel his eyes on her, but nothing would have persuaded her to be the first to speak.

'We need to talk,' he said at length. 'Rationally, I mean. What you saw this morning——'

'I already know what I saw this morning!' Anger and underlying torment savaged the interruption. 'Why bother with the excuses? You're both of you free to do as you please. And you don't have to repeat the threats. I've no intention of letting the side down now.'

The sigh was sudden and unexpected. 'Look, forget what I said on that score. There's no question of bringing in the police. You make me so mad I can't even think straight!'

'Because I see you for what you are?' Kim made no attempt to iron the scorn from her voice. 'A pity Eloise can't see it too—but then, she perhaps doesn't care.'

He made a sharp movement as if to start towards her, then stopped, features grimly set. 'We already went that route,' he said tautly. 'I'm not about to be drawn into it again.'

'Drawn?' Blue eyes blazed. 'You think I *wanted* you to rape me?'

'Scarcely rape,' he returned with sardonic inflexion. 'The struggling was minimal.'

Her throat was so tight that she almost choked on the words. 'You're an out-and-out louse, Ryan!'

'Very likely.' There was a pause. When he spoke again he sounded almost weary. 'Supposing we call a truce for the next couple of days? We'll be leaving on Monday.'

'Does your mother know?' she asked after a moment or two, trying to come to grips with suddenly conflicting emotions. 'I was under the impression they were expecting us to stay till the middle of the week.'

'That was the intention,' he said. 'Scarcely feasible now, is it?' He didn't wait for an answer. 'I'll arrange for an urgent recall Monday morning. There shouldn't be any difficulty getting seats on the evening flight. By Tuesday lunchtime you'll be safely back home with your brother, and that will be the end of it.'

'Not where your mother's concerned,' she retorted. 'She still has to go through our supposed separation and eventual divorce. Have you thought about how that's going to affect her?'

'Let me worry about it.' His tone was clipped. 'Are you going to change first, or shall I?'

Kim didn't move. 'You really don't care, do you?' she said scathingly, and saw his jaw go rigid.

'As I said, it isn't your concern.'

'It has to be someone's. It could even kill her.'

'So what would be your solution?' he demanded. 'Make the marriage real?' His lips twisted at the look on her face. 'It's an idea, I suppose.'

'A lousy one.' She was hard put to keep the tremor from her voice.

'Not if that concern you profess to feel is real.' He was moving as he spoke. 'Anyway, think about it. I'm going to take a shower.'

Kim remained where she was as the bathroom door closed behind him, mind in a turmoil. He wasn't serious, of course. He couldn't be serious! The very thought was preposterous!

## CHAPTER TEN

THE others were already down when they reached the bar. From his seat at Eloise's side, Peter got to his feet to greet them. Casual wear suited his fair good looks, Kim thought, and wondered fleetingly how her brother was spending his Christmas Eve.

The brush of Ryan's thigh against hers as they took seats side by side on one of the sofas made her quiver. Whether he had really meant that proposal of his, or had simply been taunting her, she still had no idea, because it hadn't been mentioned again. Not that it mattered so much in the long run, as the end result would be the same. Once they were back in England it was finished.

As she had suspected, Eloise made no great effort towards putting the newcomer to their group at ease. Relax he did, however, as the evening progressed and the Christmas spirit permeated the air. Any demarcation lines between parties were forgotten, the noise-level rising by the minute as wine and spirits flowed freely.

Invited to dance, Kim found Peter easy to be with, and sensed that he felt the same about her. Probably because there was no sexual attraction between them, she reflected.

'Beats the last few Christmases hands down,' he allowed when she asked him if he was enjoying the evening. 'It's like being with family again.' He tagged on lightly, 'I was going around with an English girl in Toronto for a few weeks. She'd have found this kind of affair a total loss. Nightclubs were her scene.'

'It takes all kinds,' Kim responded. 'How come you're still footloose and fancy-free? It can't be lack of opportunity.'

He gave a smiling shrug. 'Never met the right one, I guess. You don't happen to have a sister, do you?'

'Not at the last count.' She kept her tone inconsequential. 'How about Eloise?'

His expression took on a certain wry cast. 'I doubt if I'm her type.'

'What would you say *was* her type?'

The shrug came again. 'Something like your husband, maybe.'

'He's spoken for,' she said on the same light intonation. 'Which leaves the field wide open. Faint heart never won fair lady—or dark either, for that matter.'

'On the other hand, there's not much point in trying to rouse interest where none exists,' he countered. 'I'm here because Mike's a pretty thoughtful guy, no other reason.'

He was wrong about that, she was sure. Mike was desperate to have his only child settled into a permanent and happy relationship. Peter might be his idea of the perfect mate, but he couldn't force his daughter to see him the same way, no matter what subterfuge he employed.

Eloise was seated alone at the table with Ryan right now, Mike and Lydia being on the dance-floor themselves. Whatever the two of them were discussing, it had to be of a pretty serious nature, because neither was smiling. Going to rejoin them when the record finished, Kim was nonplussed by the other girl's demeanour. She looked so taut, so withdrawn.

Ryan himself was at his most unrevealing. The moment the music started up again, he got to his feet. 'Dance, Cass,' he said, and it wasn't a request.

He made no attempt to converse when they were on the floor. It was left to Kim to break the silence between them.

'Seems you might finally have blotted your copybook where Eloise is concerned,' she murmured at length. 'What on earth did you say to her?'

'I told her enough was enough,' he returned levelly. 'I should have done it before.'

'You're trying to make out there was no interest on your side?' Her tone was cutting. 'I *saw* you kissing her this morning, Ryan!'

'What you saw was Eloise making a gesture for your benefit,' he said. 'She knew you were there.' He smiled thinly. 'I'm not claiming to be blameless where she's concerned. What happened between us was regrettable. But, having said that, there was never any question of marriage.'

'You must have given her reason to think it was a possibility,' she insisted after a moment.

'Only in her own mind. I was under pressure from all sides—hence the desperation straits in the end.' He paused, voice taking on a wry quality. 'A lack of forethought on my part. I didn't take enough account of the complications.'

'Unusual for you, I'm sure.' Kim was giving no quarter. 'Why didn't you tell her the whole truth while you were about it? I doubt if she'd do anything to hurt your mother.'

'I couldn't take the risk,' he said. 'Not at this stage. The time to make that confession would be when we were really married. Obviously, it would still be something of a shock, but I don't think too great a one considering Mother already met you—and likes you.'

It took Kim a moment or two to formulate the words. 'What makes you think I'd be willing to marry you in the first place? I don't have any... feelings for you, Ryan. Apart from detestation, that is,' she added on a brittle note.

The hand at her centre back drew her closer, the other hand sliding around the back of her neck to hold her head so that he could look directly into her eyes—penetrating her defences. 'We share feelings we haven't even begun to explore yet,' he said softly. 'I'd like the chance.'

She was silent, searching his face with a kind of desperation, wanting to believe what he seemed to be saying, yet not daring to let herself. She was vibrantly aware of her body's response to his closeness—could feel her nipples peaking against the firmness of his chest. Where physical reaction was concerned, she had little power to resist, there was no denying that; it was her deeper emotions that were so confused.

'We'll talk about it later,' he added as the music came to a halt again. 'It's almost midnight.'

From his position by the stereo deck, Yves was inviting everyone to join those already on the floor in readiness for the magic moment. Ryan drew Kim a little to one side out of the main press of bodies beneath the strung net of inflated balloons awaiting release on the final stroke of twelve, his arm about her shoulders as the chimes began. She could see both Lydia and Mike on the far side of the room, but not the other two.

Ryan turned her unresistingly towards him as the last stroke rang out, bending his head to kiss her long and hard on the lips. 'Merry Christmas!' he mouthed.

It was beyond her to return the greeting; beyond her to do anything but stand there gazing at him in turmoil. There was a growing temptation to opt out from thinking at all and simply let things happen from here on in.

'We'd better go join them,' he said, with a nod of his head in the direction of the table where his mother and stepfather were now reseated.

They skirted the crowd of merry-makers still exchanging kisses and handshakes. Kim steeled herself to bend and kiss Lydia on the cheek and murmur the appropriate words, to accept Mike's hearty embrace with a smile and a further response, to watch Ryan complete the ritual and wonder if he felt any pangs of conscience at all beneath that urbane exterior.

The sighting of Eloise and Peter together amid the throng in the middle of the room came as something of a surprise. Peter himself looked a little bemused as he gazed down into the face lifted so provocatively towards his. If Eloise was using him as an anodyne against the sting of Ryan's put-down, then she should be ashamed of herself. Peter was far too nice a character to be given any run-around.

Mike was watching the pair of them too, a certain satisfaction in his expression. Kim could only hope he wasn't going to be too disappointed when his strategy failed to bear the results for which he so obviously hoped. No doubt Eloise would one day find a man to take Ryan's place, but it wouldn't be Peter Leyton. He had said it himself: he wasn't her type.

They still hadn't returned to the table when Lydia and Mike decided to call it a day. The service was at ten, Mike reminded them.

Grey eyes met blue across the table as they departed. 'Supposing we follow their example?' Ryan suggested on a note which set her heart clamouring again. 'There's a whole lot I want to say to you that can't be said here.'

There was no point in refusing, Kim acknowledged. She had to face the situation some time. What answer she was going to give, she still didn't know. Common sense prompted a definite refusal—but then common sense had played no great part in any of this so far.

They had left a couple of lamps switched on when they went down to dinner, imparting a cosy glow to the room. Ryan pulled her into his arms the moment the door was closed, kissing her into a state where she didn't know her head from her heels, and scarcely cared any more.

'You have to marry me,' he stated unequivocally. 'It's the only way I'm going to get any peace of mind where you're concerned.'

'It's too soon,' she whispered. 'We hardly know one another!'

'Enough to be going on with. The rest we can learn at leisure.' His voice roughened. 'I'm not making excuses for anything I've done, because there aren't any.

I should have explained the way it was with Eloise
this morning instead of reacting the way I did.'

'I wouldn't have believed you,' Kim admitted. 'Not
then.'

He tilted her chin to look into her eyes, turning her
bones to jelly. 'You do now, I hope?'

'Yes.' It wasn't wholly true, but she closed her mind
to any remaining doubts. Ryan wanted to marry her;
he had to want it or he'd hardly be asking. Only how
long would it last without love to back it up? Neither
physical passion nor belated filial duty was any adequate substitute.

'I need time,' she got out. 'We both need more time,
Ryan. Can't we leave things the way they are until we
at least get back home?'

For a moment he seemed about to argue the point,
then the light of opposition gave way to a reluctant
acceptance. 'It won't make any difference,' he stated,
'but if that's what you want.'

Right now, thought Kim ruefully, she wasn't sure
what she *did* want. There hadn't been a single moment
since Ryan had come into her life when she could
honestly claim to be sure of anything very much.

Wrong, came the rider as he found her mouth again.
Where this was concerned, there was no doubt at all.

The little stone-built church was crowded to the doors.
Standing at Ryan's side in the pew, Kim tried to put
the memory of his lovemaking to the back of her mind
and concentrate on the service instead, but it wasn't
easy with every fibre tuned to his male magnetism.
Most people would consider her an idiot for hesi-
tating to commit herself to what he was offering her.

Most people would probably be right too. Where else was she going to find a man who could make her feel the way Ryan made her feel?

What it all came down to, she supposed, was lack of trust. He might tell himself he wanted marriage now—he might even believe it—but would he still want it in a year or so when the novelty had worn off? Words like separation and divorce came too easily to his lips.

Which brought her round to Lydia. She would have to be told the truth eventually, of course. The alternative held too many obstacles to even contemplate. Yet was the realisation of her son's duplicity liable to put any less strain on her than the supposed break-up might have done?

She was going around in circles and getting precisely nowhere, Kim acknowledged wryly at that point. Why not follow her own advice and leave things until they were back in England and free of present pressures? Playing Cassandra was more than enough to be going on with.

Snow was falling when they emerged, coating the shoulders of the party occupying the passing horse-drawn sleigh. Just like a picture postcard, thought Kim, viewing the brightly decorated shop windows and house-fronts through the gently drifting flakes.

Wrapped in lilac mink, Eloise was still holding Peter in thrall. How long she would keep it up was anyone's guess, but he appeared to be enjoying the experience. They made a good-looking couple, Kim had to admit. Perhaps they might even finish up hitting it off after all.

As Ryan drove back to the Lodge, she surreptitiously fingered the gold bracelet Ryan had presented her with before breakfast. If she didn't marry him, he would have to take it back, of course, along with all the other things. She couldn't contemplate keeping it.

He had professed himself delighted with his own present—and expressed his thanks in his own inimitable way. How could she not say yes to him? she asked herself now, reliving those moments. Wasn't it worth taking a chance?

'Are you still planning on arranging that phone call for Monday?' she asked, and felt his glance.

'Do you want me to?'

'It might be advisable. Among other things, it will give me time to organise myself before I start the new job.'

'I'd forgotten about that,' he admitted. 'Monday it is, then.' There was a pause before he added, 'What other things?'

'I'd have difficulty keeping up the pretence until the weekend,' Kim confessed. 'I feel such a fraud!'

'I'm the guilty party,' he returned. 'There's no blame attached to you.'

'I could have refused.'

The strong mouth took on a slant. 'Not the way I stacked the deck. Too late for apologies. All I can do is try to make up for it.'

Her eyes were on the lean brown hands holding the wheel, recalling the exquisite sensitivity of those well-tended fingertips as they moved over her. She moistened suddenly dry lips, clamping down heavily on the urge to reach out and run her own fingertips along the muscular thigh. There was a time and a place, and this was neither.

'I feel the same way,' he said softly without looking at her. 'I felt it the first time I laid eyes on you.'

'You said you didn't have any designs on my body,' she reminded him, and saw his mouth tilt again.

'So I'm an inveterate liar. What I didn't allow for was the degree of involvement. There's a whole lot more to you than your looks, Kim. I didn't even start to plumb the depths yet. Leaving everything else aside, I'm pretty sure we could make a go of it.'

The urge to give way was almost too great to resist, but a small corner of her mind managed to retain some measure of judgement. 'We've done little but fight since we met,' she pointed out. 'That's hardly a good basis for marriage.'

His laugh held a genuine amusement. 'A yes-woman wouldn't have the same appeal. You've put me through the hoop with a vengeance. Not that I haven't asked for it. Sensitivity was never my forte.' He paused as if waiting for some reply, sobering a little when it failed to materialise. 'I won't let you go, Kim,' he added levelly. 'Not without one hell of a struggle, at any rate!'

Her pulses quickened as he brought the car to a halt at the roadside. The snow was coming faster and thicker, visibility down to a few hundred feet.

'We're going to be driving blind if we're not careful,' she said thickly. 'Ryan, I——'

'We don't move from here until you agree to marry me,' he stated. 'I don't care how long it takes.' The grey eyes were resolute, matching the determined set of his jaw. 'Or *what* it takes.'

She made no move as he took off the fox hat. The feel of his fingers in her hair tingled every nerve in her body. He started at her temple, lips so unbelievably light and delicate, moving with slow deliberation to kiss each eye, then down over the curve of her cheekbone to the fluttering pulse-point just below her ear. The tremors started from way down deep, gathering strength as they extended through her body and making it hard to breathe. Lips half parted, eyes half closed, she could no more have drawn away from that caressing contact than fly.

She was almost feverish with desire by the time he reached her mouth, but still he didn't hurry, teasing her lips with little nibbling bites until she could barely contain herself. The male scent of him was an arousal in itself. She brought up her hands to his face, feeling the hardness of bone, the warm texture of his skin, the strong firm line of his jaw—moving on down to his shoulders, so broad and powerful beneath the sheepskin coat, sliding blindly around his neck to bring herself up closer to him. Enclosed within the layers of clothing, her breasts ached for more intimate contact. Impossible, of course, with the air inside the car already chilling.

'Say yes,' he murmured against her lips. '*Say* it, Kim!'

The word came without prompting. The effort would have been in saying otherwise. This emotion they shared might not be love as she had always thought of it, but it had to be close. From here, they could only become closer.

'And not before time,' he growled, but he was smiling. 'A few more minutes and we'd both need thawing out!'

She sat back in her seat as he restarted the engine. None of this was really happening, she told herself. She'd had dreams before where she knew she was dreaming yet couldn't waken up.

Only Ryan was real enough; no dream character could feel the way he felt, do the things he did. She had to stop doubting and start accepting.

They reached the Lodge to find everyone drinking coffee in the lobby while they opened the general family presents which had been left under the tree. Kim had a hard time hiding her discomfiture on seeing the soft cashmere sweater from Lydia and Mike.

If it had been possible to confess to the truth there and then she would have done it, but news of that nature was hardly scheduled to enhance the spirit of Christmas. As Ryan had said, better after they could at least claim to be legitimately married.

Eloise had bought them a joint present in the shape of a beautifully framed print of Old Montreal, for which she accepted thanks with an oddly ironic little smile. There were also gifts from Peter for them all.

'The very least I could do by way of thanks for letting me join the family party,' he disclaimed in answer to Lydia's remonstrance. His eyes went to Eloise, expression only too readable. 'I'd have been pretty much on my own otherwise.'

'You're welcome any time,' Mike assured him comfortably. 'I dare say Cass and Ryan will be coming over again before the winter's over. We can organise another weekend up here.' He glanced at his stepson for confirmation. 'Yes?'

'Fine with us,' Ryan assured him with an ease Kim wished she could only emulate. By the time they visited again, the truth would need to be known. No matter how it was put, it had to cause some ill feeling.

All the tables in the dining-room had been pushed together in one long line for lunch, and magnificently set. There were crackers and paper hats for everybody.

Looking at Ryan, entering into the spirit of the occasion in a Napoleonic bicorne, Kim felt a sudden swelling of emotion. It could be good between them if she let it. All it needed was a little faith.

# CHAPTER ELEVEN

THE snow petered out overnight, leaving a world of dazzling whiteness under the clear blue skies of morning. This time there were others already waiting for the chair-lift to open when they reached the station.

Eloise was different this morning, Kim reflected, listening to the other girl chatting casually with Peter as they stood in line. There was still some slight frigidity where Ryan was concerned, but only noticeable to anyone in the know. To herself, she had been almost friendly.

Meeting Ryan's eyes, she felt the familiar curling sensation deep in the pit of her stomach, the swift leap of her pulses. Had that uninhibited creature last night really been her? That slow, reflective smile of his said yes. The best Christmas present a man ever had, he had called her. She wished they were alone together right now.

Tomorrow they would be leaving for home. It would be a relief in many ways, although there were going to be other difficulties to face on arrival. Tony, for instance. How was he likely to react to the knowledge that she was to marry Ryan Bentley?

With definite approval, after the initial surprise, came the dry thought. It could hardly be a disadvantage to have the company president for a brother-in-law. Not that Ryan would be likely to see him in any benevolent light. Another attempt to utilise company funds would bring retribution regardless; she was pretty sure of that.

They ski'd the Black run again, only this time it was Eloise and Peter who went on ahead. Kim was delighted to get down to the treeline in only four turns. All it took was practice, Ryan commented.

'We could honeymoon in Switzerland, if you like,' he added casually. 'Or would you prefer somewhere warmer for a change?'

Kim hadn't thought about a honeymoon; she hadn't even considered the actual wedding as yet. 'I shan't be able to take time off from my job,' she said, wondering how soon he had in mind. Her laugh sounded just a little bit forced. 'We'll have to make this do instead.'

Dark brows lifted. 'I thought all women wanted a traditional honeymoon.'

'I'm not all women,' she rejoined, not caring to add that a traditional honeymoon went with a traditional wedding, and theirs was quite some way from that. She had done a lot of thinking since yesterday, and come to the conclusion that, while his professed feelings for her might be genuine enough, it was debatable whether they would have led to a proposal of marriage under normal circumstances. When the situation was looked at realistically, he had left himself with little real choice in the end.

His shrug made light of the subject. 'We can sort that aspect out later. Are you ready to make the next stretch?'

We just sorted it, she thought stubbornly, positioning herself for the off. A new job could hardly be put aside to suit. In fact, if experience was anything to go by, she was going to be putting in extra hours just to keep on top of it.

The others had waited for them at the bottom of the run. Eloise had something of a sparkle in her eye, while Peter looked as if life had taken a distinct turn for the better.

'I fancy a coffee,' declared the Canadian girl as they made towards the lift. 'How about you, Cass?'

That name didn't help, Kim acknowledged ruefully. It took an effort to keep her tone casual. 'Good idea.'

Eloise looked back at the two men. 'You don't have to hang about for us. We'll see you here when you get down again. OK?'

Ryan gave her a measured scrutiny before inclining his head in agreement. 'OK.'

Seated in the warmth of the café with the steaming mugs in front of them, Kim searched her mind for some topic of conversation that wouldn't sound too contrived. It was Eloise herself, however, who set the ball rolling.

'I want to say sorry for acting the way I've acted,' she proffered. 'You didn't deserve it.'

Little did she know, thought Kim, feeling worse than ever. 'It doesn't matter,' she mumbled.

'Yes, it does.' The other was obviously resolved to have her say. 'What happened between Ryan and me was entirely my fault.'

Kim said softly, 'I hardly think you raped him.'

'Not so very far from it,' with a faint smile. 'I'd spent many frustrating years waiting for him to see me as something more than a kid sister. The one time he did was because I left him no option. Falling into the drift was no accident. I planned every detail of that afternoon.'

'He could still have said no,' Kim insisted, and saw the smile come again.

'There are circumstances under which any man would find the ability seriously curtailed. That power is in every woman's hands, Cass, if she dares use it. I dared because I was desperate.'

'I'm sorry.' Kim didn't know what else to say. 'I really am sorry, Eloise.'

The shrug was brief. 'I'll get over it. I only hope I haven't caused any rift between the two of you. I was eaten up with jealousy of you because you're his wife.'

'I'm not.' Kim couldn't stand any more. If Eloise could bare her soul this way, she could scarcely do less herself. 'Not yet, anyway,' she added unhappily. 'And my name isn't Cassandra, it's Kimberly—Kim for short.'

Eloise was looking at her with a stunned expression. 'I'm not sure I understand,' she said.

There was no going back now. Neither did Kim want to. The relief of being able to tell someone the truth at last was tremendous. 'Ryan pretended to have got married in order to stop his mother from badgering him to find a wife,' she said. 'Then when she became ill, he had to find someone to play the part. It was only supposed to be for a few days at first, but it didn't work out that way.'

Shock had given way to a wry recognition. 'Not only his mother,' Eloise observed. 'He had to convince me too. A drastic measure, but effective.' Her gaze sharpened a little. 'You said not yet. Does that mean what it appears to mean?'

Kim nodded. 'We're going to be married when we get back home.'

'A condition you made?'

Blue eyes sprang into sudden brilliant life. 'No!' She caught herself up again to add on a more restrained note, 'Obviously, Lydia is going to have to know the truth some time, but he hopes she'll accept it better if we've at least made some effort to put things right in the meantime.'

Eloise eyed her contemplatively. 'But you do *want* to marry him, don't you?'

The hesitation was brief enough to be almost non-existent. 'Of course. Who wouldn't?' She caught herself up, flushing a little at the gaffe. 'That wasn't meant to sound snide.'

Eloise smiled and shook her head. 'Forget it. I may have had some idea of causing trouble between you, but I gave up any real hope of having him for myself some time ago.' She paused, tone altering. 'It might be best if you left it to me to break the news once you've done the deed. I'll be better placed to choose the right moment.'

Kim could see the sense in that immediately, even if it did appear to be opting out of responsibility to a certain extent. It would mean that Ryan would have to know she had told his stepsister the whole story, of course, but that was only anticipating the inevitable.

'You're being very understanding,' she said gratefully. 'I'm not sure I could have done the same if the positions had been reversed.'

'A way of making up for a bad start to our relationship,' came the answer. 'I want us to be friends, Cass—I mean, Kim.'

'You'd better stick to Cass for now,' Kim reminded her. 'It will only be until tomorrow. Ryan's arranging for an urgent call home.' She pulled a face. 'One lie begets another.'

'A tangled web,' Eloise agreed. 'But we'll straighten it out between us.'

Kim studied the finely boned face beneath its smooth cap of dark hair. 'What really made you change your mind?' she asked curiously.

'Come to my senses, you mean?' Slender shoulders lifted. 'Ryan left little unsaid on Christmas Eve. Once I got over the initial affront, I had to agree with him.'

'And Peter?' Kim ventured.

The smile this time was softer. 'I'm beginning to think I might have been blind in more than one direction. Dad introduced us months ago, but I didn't pay any attention. Pete has hidden depths.'

'He's very good-looking.'

'Isn't he, though? Knocks Ryan into a cocked hat!' Just for a second there was pain in the dark eyes, swiftly banished. 'Talking of Ryan, I'd advise not telling him I know about it all until you're well on your way home. He might not like the idea of me breaking the news in his stead, although, short of making another trip over, I'm not sure how he intended doing it himself.'

'I've no idea either,' Kim admitted. She leaned back in her chair, feeling better than she had done in days. A trouble shared was a trouble halved—trite but true. With Eloise's aid enlisted, nothing seemed quite as bad any more.

'So tell me about yourself,' the other girl invited. 'The real you, I mean.'

They were talking like old friends by the time the two men returned. The latter took time out to drink a coffee themselves before the four of them went back up for the final run of the morning. Once or twice, Kim caught a quizzical look in Ryan's eye as he registered the altered atmosphere between her and Eloise. She kept her own expression bland, and hoped he wouldn't ask any awkward questions. There would be plenty of time on the plane to tell him what they had planned, though he could surely only be relieved to have the problem taken care of.

Lunchtime found Mike with a smile on his face like a Cheshire cat as he watched his daughter talking animatedly with the man he had invited here for her. Lydia looked pleased about it too. So far as she was concerned, everything had worked out quite well. All Kim could hope for was a swift and not too traumatic adjustment to the new order when it was presented. Eloise would do her best to minimise the impact, she was sure. The other's feelings for her stepmother were undisguisedly supportive.

With regard to her own feelings, she was still in a state of flux, one minute exhilarated at the thought of marrying Ryan, the next plagued by doubts again. There was so much they still had to learn about each other. She didn't even know where he lived as yet.

'I have an apartment in town, and a house in Surrey left me by my grandmother,' he acknowledged when she put the question later while they were getting ready to go out again. 'Silverwood's a listed building. I'm in the process of restoring it to former glories. I reckon another six months' work before it's ready to be lived in.' He paused as if awaiting some comment, glancing her way when she failed to make it. 'I plan on using the place at weekends. I don't fancy the hassle of daily commuting.'

'No way to start the morning,' Kim agreed lightly. 'I gather your apartment will take two?'

His smile was slow. 'Right through to the double bed. You can view it Wednesday after we both recover from jet lag. It's always worse going west to east. Something to do with the magnetic poles.' He paused again, tone altering. 'If I get straight on to it, Friday should be OK.'

Her heart jerked. 'For what?'

'The register office.'

She said huskily, 'Why the rush?'

'There's no reason to hang around,' he returned levelly. 'I want to get things straightened out. We can go somewhere for the weekend at least. How about Paris?'

How about leaving me room to breathe? she wanted to ask, but the words stuck in her throat. If she was going to marry him at all, it might just as well be sooner as later, she supposed. And the quieter, the better.

'Surprise me,' she suggested, striving for normality, and saw the smile come again.

'I'll do my level best.'

The weather stayed good all afternoon. This time, Kim found herself tackling the Black run without a qualm. No sport offered greater exhilaration than this downhill swoop, she thought exultantly, following close in Ryan's wake. She had some way to go yet to match his style and expertise, but she had time on her side.

'If you're here next winter, we'll have to go further afield,' Eloise remarked on the way back to the Lodge.

'The Mont Tremblant slopes are a real challenge.' Her gaze moved to Ryan, losing just a fraction of its animation in the process. 'You'll be coming over fairly regularly again, I imagine?'

'As often as we can,' he agreed. 'Even if it's only for a long weekend.'

Only someone like Ryan, thought Kim, could contemplate hopping across the Atlantic for a weekend. As his wife, she would need to cultivate the same attitude. That might be the most difficult part yet.

Preparing for dinner, he said casually, 'You and Eloise seem to be getting along rather well.'

'We are,' Kim agreed, concentrating on the lipstick she was applying. 'We decided it was better to be friends than enemies.' The pause was deliberate, and just a little bit malicious. 'After all, we do have some things in common.'

'It happened before we even met,' came the brusque response. 'I'm not going to spend the rest of my life doing penance for it.'

She was already regretting the remark. It hadn't been necessary. She could see him through the mirror, tall and lean in the tailored brown trousers and toning shirt he had elected to wear tonight, dark hair needing a brush after his shower. The familiar warmth stirred her blood.

'Sorry,' she said.

Grey eyes softened a fraction as he looked back at her. Coming over to where she sat at the dressing-table mirror, he drew her to her feet to kiss her with a reassuring thoroughness.

'I'd suggest we gave dinner a miss and stayed up here if it weren't our last evening,' he said before letting go of her. 'We've a lot to learn about each other.'

And plenty of time to do it in, Kim thought, feeling suddenly positive. Whether it was reciprocated or not, she loved this man.

The arranged telephone call came through at eight. Returning to the breakfast table, Ryan made the announcement with suitable regret. Nothing too drastic, he said, but there was a board meeting called for Tuesday afternoon. He'd got straight on to the airport and reserved seats for the evening flight.

'You'll have to take the Cadillac and leave it to be picked up later,' said Mike, turning to the practicalities. 'If you leave here after lunch, you'll have plenty of time. No point in hanging around the departure lounge any longer than you have to.'

'There's no reason why Cass should have to go today too, is there?' asked Lydia. 'If you're going to be tied up with business . . .'

'It's a nice thought,' Kim said quickly, 'but I hate travelling alone.' She caught Eloise's glance across the table, grateful for the empathy she saw there. If Ryan had been serious in suggesting they were married this coming Friday, the whole situation could be cleared up by next weekend. She smiled at the older woman. 'We'll be coming back.'

Most of the packing had already been done in anticipation. Finishing off in the bedroom, she said wryly, 'I feel absolutely rotten leaving like this.'

'It's needs must,' Ryan answered. 'You said it yourself: the longer we stay, the more difficult it gets.'

'We could confess,' she ventured, and saw his jawline harden.

'Telling them now would only spoil a good Christmas.'

'So how do you propose doing it?' she challenged. 'By letter?'

He shook his head. 'When the time comes, it will be in person.'

'So it won't be immediate?'

'No,' he admitted.

She said softly, 'In which case, why rush the wedding?'

He studied her for a long moment with unreadable expression. 'Why wait?' he asked. 'You think your mother might be persuaded to come over from Australia for it?'

It was Kim's turn to shake her head, smile rueful. 'She wouldn't leave her family.'

'Then why wait?' he repeated. 'New Year's Eve seems an ideal time to start a new life—especially as you're going to be tied up with the new job. We can take off for Paris in the afternoon, and stay till Sunday.'

'Supposing the register office can't take us Friday?'

'Then it will have to be Thursday,' came the unmoved response. 'Do you need any help closing that case?'

She answered in the affirmative, standing back to allow him access. It was going to be a hectic few days, with Tony not the least of her problems, yet she had to acknowledge a certain gladness that she hadn't managed to persuade Ryan to wait. Once she was married to him, everything would be different, the ring on her finger no longer a sham. It was a stimulating thought.

# CHAPTER TWELVE

THEY left the Lodge at three in good clear weather, arriving at Mirabel in time to have a coffee and sandwich before boarding the plane.

Settling down for the six-hour flight, Kim wondered how long it would be before she could take first-class privileges for granted the way Ryan did. Her whole lifestyle was about to undergo a radical change.

With home so close, she had to start sparing a thought for her brother. There was no way he was going to be able to manage the rent for the flat on his salary. Not unless he changed *his* lifestyle. Her fault mostly for carrying him for so long, she knew, but being aware of it didn't help now. She would simply have to go on subbing him until he found somewhere he could afford, that was all.

She slept after the film, wakening to the breakfast-tray and a heavy head.

'Another hour,' Ryan advised. He rubbed a hand over his jaw with a grimace. 'I'll feel more human after a shave and a change of shirt.'

Kim would have given a great deal for a hot shower, but that was asking a bit too much even of first-class, she supposed. She settled for a wash and brush-up instead, returning to her seat feeling brighter if not wholly renewed.

'It's strange to think they'll all be in bed and fast asleep still at the Lodge,' she remarked when Ryan came back looking as fresh as if he'd spent the night in a comfortable bed himself. 'I can never accustom myself to the time differences.' She hesitated before taking the plunge. 'Eloise knows about us, Ryan.'

His head came sharply round. 'How the devil——?'

'I told her,' she interposed.

Eyes steely, tone grim, he said, 'Why?'

'It just came out.' Kim refused to be thrown by his obvious anger. 'She understood your reasons. She even offered to break it to your mother when the time comes.'

'Did she, though?' There was no softening of either expression or voice. 'And what else did the two of you decide for me?'

'It wasn't like that,' she appealed. 'Eloise simply wants to help. I think she might be right in thinking it would be better coming from her. She's on the spot; she can judge the moment.'

'And leave me looking the kind of louse who can't take care of his own dirty work?' He shook his head, mouth a thin straight line. 'I got myself into this, I'll get myself out.'

Kim felt in no position to argue the pros and cons of the situation. It was Ryan's decision to make. Whichever way it was handled, Lydia had to be told the truth eventually. One could only trust to providence that she'd suffer no ill effects.

They landed at seven o'clock, went through Immigration and Customs without bother, and emerged into a light snow-shower and a temperature almost laughably warm after the rigours of a Canadian winter.

Ryan had the taxi drop Kim off first. He carried her suitcase up to the flat, showing little reaction when Tony proved to be still in bed.

'The holiday isn't over yet,' he said. 'We'll tell him the news tonight.'

'I think I should prepare the way first,' Kim asserted. 'He is under the impression I've been staying with friends in Devon, after all.'

Ryan's smile held a certain irony. 'Seems we're well suited in most directions. What exactly *will* you tell him?'

'Just the bare bones,' she said. 'I helped you out with a problem, and we...'

'The term is "fell in love",' he supplied as she hesitated. 'It happens all the time.' He bent his head to press a brief, unsatisfying kiss to her lips. 'I'll be here around seven. We'll eat out.'

He was gone before she could come up with any answer. Turning back into the flat, she thought how dark and cramped it looked by comparison with what she had become used to these past ten days. Delusions of grandeur already, she told herself wryly.

The place was a mess. After taking her things through to her bedroom, she made an immediate start on clearing away some of the accumulated debris of what appeared to be a whole series of parties.

Dirty glasses littered every available surface. By the time she had cleared them all into the kitchen, and emptied the overflowing ashtrays, it was gone ten o'clock. There wasn't much point in going to bed, she decided. She would be unlikely to sleep with Tony still to face. She made coffee instead, sitting at the tiny kitchen table to drink it while she tried to sort out exactly what she *was* going to say to her brother.

'I'm going to marry your president,' seemed just a little too bald, although she had no intention of going into too much detail either. What Tony didn't know he couldn't blab about to anyone else.

The sound of movement from the adjoining bedroom straightened her back in anticipation. The first thing he always wanted after a binge was a recuperating black coffee. She had herself well in hand by the time he appeared in the kitchen doorway.

Tony had a towel wrapped about the lower half of his body. Slimmer in build than Ryan, and lacking the golden tan of the latter's skin, he none the less brought memory alive in a way that made her ache. He looked totally nonplussed to see her sitting there.

'I wasn't expecting you back for a few days yet,' he said. 'You must have been late getting in. The party didn't finish till gone three.'

'I came in an hour ago,' she said.

His brow creased. 'Why such an early train?'

'I didn't come by train.' When it came right down to it, she decided at that moment, there was only one way to do this. She had removed the wedding-ring earlier. Now she held out her hand with the diamond hoop glinting there. 'Congratulations would be in order.'

It took a moment to sink in. When he finally found his voice he sounded totally confused. 'Who? I didn't even realise you were seeing anybody seriously.'

She took a deep breath before saying it. 'Ryan Bentley.'

Confusion crystallised into disbelief. 'Some joke!'

'It isn't a joke,' she denied. 'I've been with him in Canada over Christmas, meeting his family.'

'But . . . how?' The blue eyes looked stunned. 'You were in Devon. You phoned me.'

'From Canada.' She made an apologetic gesture. 'I had to be sure before I told you. It happened so quickly. Ryan caught me altering the records that night, and it just . . . went from there.'

Tony drew out the other chair and sat down as if his legs had gone suddenly weak. 'Let me get this quite straight,' he said. 'The company president caught you falsifying records and decided you'd make the perfect wife. Is that what you're telling me?'

'Near enough,' she acknowledged. 'It happens that way sometimes.' She made an effort to smile. 'Love at first sight, et cetera.'

Expression bemused, he said, 'Ryan Bentley! Who'd have imagined it?' Realisation sprang sudden alarm in his eyes. 'He knows what I did?'

'Yes, but he's willing to forget it, providing it doesn't happen again.'

'No chance!' The avowal was emphatic. 'Once was more than enough.' He was getting over the shock now, beginning to recognise the possible advantages. 'There's more to you than I'd ever have thought, Kim, landing a catch like that. You'll have half the women in town ready to scratch your eyes out from sheer envy! When do I get to see him?'

Only her brother could contemplate meeting the man who could have put him in gaol with such magnificent aplomb, thought Kim drily, relieved to have the worst of it over. He might come up with one or two awkward questions later, but it had proved surprisingly easy in the end. She was becoming quite an accomplished liar herself. If nothing else, she and Ryan had a facile tongue in common.

There was still the matter of the wedding itself to deal with, came the reminder. Only not right this minute. Let it wait awhile.

'Tonight,' she said. 'He'll be here around seven to pick me up for dinner.'

'Great! We must have a bottle of champagne to celebrate.' Any post-party bleariness had long since dispersed. 'Providing you can let me have a sub till the end of the month, that is. I blew my last fifty on the party.'

All systems normal, Kim reflected. He was going to get the shock of his life when he realised how soon he would be losing his source of extra support. Not that it would be difficult to find someone to share both the flat and allied expenses with him, if it came to that.

He went out after lunch, promising to be back with the champagne in good time to meet his future brother-in-law. Kim spent the afternoon unpacking, then took a long, relaxing bath and let her mind drift back over the past days and nights—particularly the nights. Mrs Ryan Bentley. Would she ever get used to the idea?

She would have to tell the personnel office of her change of name first thing, she realised. It was going to look very odd, but it couldn't be helped. Starting a new job at a time like this was far from ideal, but there was little she could do about that either. She would simply have to take it in her stride. Good practice for future crises. Keeping a cool head in the face of adversity was what it was all about.

When the telephone rang around four-thirty, she was halfway through painting her nails. Cursing inwardly, she went to gingerly lift the receiver. It was almost sure to be for Tony anyway.

The voice on the other end of the line sounded clear enough to be coming from the next room instead of three thousand miles away. 'Kim, it's Eloise.'

Surprise kept her from answering for a moment. When she did it was to say irrelevantly, 'How did you know my number?'

'You told me your real name and whereabouts you lived that afternoon in the café. It was enough for directories to find you.' There was a pause before she went on, 'That opportunity I was talking about cropped up last night. Too good a one to miss. *Marâtre* provided the opening herself. Apparently she suspected all wasn't quite as it should be between you and Ryan. She was worried you might already be breaking up and trying to hide it from her. Anyway, to cut it short, I decided it was better she knew the truth now than keep on thinking that way, so I told her all of it.'

Kim was struggling to view the development objectively. *'Everything?'* she asked with delicate emphasis, and heard the wry little laugh.

'Well, maybe not quite. She knew all along how I felt about Ryan, but there's no way I'd want her to know how far I went to try and get him. She believes the two of us drove him into a corner between us.' The laugh came again. 'Sons can never really do any serious wrong in a mother's eyes, can they? Anyway, she's taken it all extremely well, considering. One thing she emphasised, Kim. You must neither of you feel obliged to do anything you don't really want to do on her account.'

It took Kim a moment to find the words. 'Have you been in touch with Ryan himself yet?'

'No, I'm leaving that to you.' Another pause, an added emphasis. 'I hope you decide to go ahead anyway. Let us know as soon as you work it out.'

Kim replaced the receiver slowly and carefully. She felt oddly detached. Ryan's main reason for suggesting marriage in the first place—and hers for agreeing, if it came to that—had been for his mother's sake. With that pressure removed, they were both at liberty to think again. All she had to do was tell him he was off the hook.

She was ready and waiting in the slim-skirted, black jersey dress she had picked at random from her wardrobe when Tony returned at six-thirty bearing a bottle of Moët et Chandon.

'You look a bit pale,' he observed with brotherly candour. 'I'd give the blusher another outing, if I were you. Can't have the man changing his mind at this stage.'

As a joke, it fell decidedly flat, although Kim managed to summon a hint of a smile. He could be nearer the truth than he imagined.

Ryan arrived promptly at seven, looking devastating in a dark grey suit and white silk shirt that accentuated his tan, a lightweight overcoat over an arm. His greeting was curtailed by Tony's entry from the kitchen with the opened bottle of champagne and three glasses on a tray.

'Hope it's cold enough,' said the latter cheerfully. 'It's only had half an hour in the fridge.'

For someone who had embezzled a fair sum of money from the very company in which the man facing him owned majority shares, his nerve was without equal, Kim thought, unsurprised to see the sardonic lift of Ryan's eyebrow.

'It's the gesture that matters,' he returned with a creditable lack of sarcasm. He accepted the glass Tony poured for him, looking across to where Kim was standing with a smile on his lips. 'Shouldn't you be over here with me while your brother calls the toast?'

She moved with reluctance to stand beside him, steeling herself for his touch as he slid his arm about her shoulders to draw her closer. None of it was necessary any more, but she could scarcely tell him here in front of Tony. The emotive scent of his aftershave aroused too many memories. She would have given anything at that moment never to have set eyes on Ryan Bentley.

'To a long and happy marriage!' intoned the younger man. 'I might even get around to trying it myself one day,' he added blandly after drinking to the toast. 'When I can afford it, that is.'

'It's said two can live as cheaply as one,' returned Ryan, equally blandly. 'You'll be relieved to hear I decided to let you keep your job, by the way. Only, step out of line again and I'll be down on you like a ton of bricks. Understood?'

He had asked for it, Kim acknowledged, watching her brother undergo a sudden metamorphosis of attitude, and Ryan wasn't the man to let him get away with it. What he was, she thought achingly, was the man she loved and might very well be going to lose.

They departed a few minutes later, leaving behind a very much subdued young man. Ryan was driving his own car tonight—a silver Mercedes that glinted in the chill moonlight as they walked towards it.

'Why aren't you wearing the fox?' he asked, sensing her shiver as the wind whipped round the corner of the block and cut through her black woollen coat. 'It's cold enough even here.'

'It's only on loan,' she said. 'I didn't want to risk it any further.'

'We took it on approval,' he corrected. 'I'd say it had been approved, wouldn't you?'

'I suppose so.' She was wretched, wanting to say what she had to say, yet dreading to hear what she didn't want to hear. 'Where are we going?' she asked as he opened the passenger door of the car for her. 'I mean, which restaurant?'

'None,' he said. 'I thought we'd kill two birds with one stone and have dinner at the apartment. Tomorrow, I'll take you down to see the house. You might have one or two ideas you'd like to incorporate yourself.'

After dinner, Kim promised herself, seizing on the reprieve. Just a couple more hours of illusion before she offered him back his freedom of choice.

The apartment was in Knightsbridge: a suite of rooms occupying the upper floor of a gracious Georgian house. Superbly decorated and furnished it still managed to retain the feel of a home. A wall of bookshelves in the living-room held titles Kim itched to take down and peruse.

'I collect first editions,' Ryan acknowledged when she commented on a section held behind glass. 'Would you like a drink before we eat?'

'A gimlet, please.' She waited until he brought the gin and lime juice across to ask curiously, 'Who's cooking dinner?'

His grin softened the contours of his face. 'Did you think I was expecting you to set to? My housekeeper left everything ready. All we have to do is help ourselves.'

'Does she live in?'

'No, she comes on a daily basis. And, in case you're wondering,' he added drily, 'she's also in her fifties and weighs in at around twelve stone.'

'I wasn't,' Kim denied, wishing that was all she had to concern her at the moment. The more she saw of Ryan's lifestyle, the more she recognised his self-sufficiency. He didn't need a wife, that was evident.

The dining-room was reached through an archway, the table ready laid for two. Ryan lit the tall cream-coloured candles in the silver candelabrum, switching off the main lights to leave just the golden glow.

'Cosier this way,' he said. 'I'll show you the rest of the place after we've eaten. It's quite extensive.'

She could well believe it. This was a whole other world.

There was melon and Parma ham to start, followed by a beautifully prepared duck à l'orange which needed just a short burst in the microwave to come up succulently hot and savoury. Kim tried to do justice to it, but found every mouthful an effort. The accompanying wine helped a little. She needed some kind of fortification before she told him of Eloise's phone call.

She refused dessert altogether, settling for coffee and a brandy and a head beginning to feel distinctly light. Ryan made no comment, but she was aware of a certain speculation in the grey eyes from time to time as she skittered from subject to subject. When he asked if she was ready to take the promised tour of the apartment, she was only too ready to put off the moment of truth a little longer.

As he had said, the place was extensive. Apart from the living-room, dining-room and well-fitted kitchen, there were two sizeable bedrooms, each with its own en-suite bathroom, a study which could double as a third bedroom if required, and a lobby big enough to take a chesterfield in addition to the long-case clock and occasional table.

Ryan left his own bedroom till last. Decorated in dark green hessian with touches of gold in the lamp shades and drapes, it was an essentially masculine abode, yet saved from austerity by the several paintings gracing the walls.

'Anyone I'm likely to know?' asked Kim, studying an oil of a reclining nude with her back turned.

'It's an Ingres,' he advised. 'Whoever she was, she's been dead a long time.' He had moved up behind her, so close that she could feel his breath stirring her hair. The touch of his hands on her shoulders made her quiver. 'You're like a cat on hot bricks,' he said on an altered note. 'You have been all night. Why, Kim?'

'I've got something to tell you,' she admitted, her voice low toned. 'I should have done it earlier.'

'So tell me,' he invited without inflexion.

'Eloise telephoned this afternoon,' she said. 'Apparently she told your mother the whole story last night.'

The hands on her shoulders tautened painfully, though he still made no attempt to turn her about. 'And?'

'It's all right. She understood why you did it, and she's forgiven you.' Kim kept her voice level by sheer will-power. 'So, you see, there's no reason why we should have to get married after all.'

'Does that mean you changed your mind?' The question came very quietly.

'It isn't a case of that, is it?' she said thickly. 'If it hadn't been for your mother's condition, things would never have got as far in the first place.'

'And if it hadn't been for your brother's misdeeds, we might never have met at all.' His voice had softened, his hands moving to curve round her neck beneath the bright fall of her hair. 'Kim, when I asked you to marry me it wasn't just for my mother's sake, it was for mine too. My motives may not have been so very pure when I blackmailed you into going out there with me, but you soon changed all that. I realise you don't feel quite the same way about me as yet, but *I* aim to change that. The one thing I can't countenance is losing you.'

She felt as if her heart were being squeezed in a vice. She could hardly get the words out. 'Which way *do* you feel, Ryan?'

He turned her then, looking down into her upturned face with an expression in his eyes that made her catch her breath. 'I love you,' he said roughly. 'I never told any woman that before.' One hand came up to smooth her cheek, lingering along the line of her jaw. 'I want to see this face on the pillow beside me when I wake up every morning, feel your lovely, warm, tempting body close to mine. I'm no holy Joe, and I'm unlikely to become one overnight, but I can promise you commitment where the two of us are concerned.'

There was a great surging elation spreading through her, an urge to laugh out loud, to shout from the rooftops. No more pretence, no more play-acting, this was real!

'Make love to me,' she said with sudden urgency, no longer bothering to conceal the glowing emotion in her eyes. 'Here in your room, in your bed!'

'Our bed,' he corrected, swinging her up readily into his arms. 'The one we'll be sharing for the next fifty years or more, God willing!'

It was the best yet, Kim thought mistily some time later when they lay replete and enervated in each other's arms. To make love with love surpassed everything. She had never felt so totally, wonderfully, securely happy in her whole life before.

'You still haven't said it,' Ryan murmured without lifting his head from its resting place on her breast. 'Not in so many words. I want to hear it from you, Kim.'

Fingers threading the thick dark hair, she said softly, 'I love you, Ryan. I tried every which way not to, but it caught up with me in the end. I dare say I may even die of it eventually.'

'Not before I give you permission,' he growled, coming up to kiss her with fast-rejuvenating passion on the lips. 'And that won't be while I'm alive and kicking.'

'What about the wedding?' she asked after another lengthy interlude. 'Are you still thinking of Friday?'

'It's all arranged,' he said. 'Ten o'clock in the morning, the Paris flight at three. Time for a celebration lunch between times.' He lifted his head to add with sudden diffidence. 'You weren't hankering after a white wedding with all the trimmings, were you?'

'No,' she told him truthfully. 'Apart from Tony, I wouldn't have any family to invite, and your mother certainly couldn't make the journey.'

'That's all right, then,' relaxing again. 'Nothing to wait for. We'll phone Mother tomorrow and put her mind at rest.'

He was right, she thought, there *was* nothing to wait for. Tony was old enough to look after himself, and capable of finding a flatmate. She would tell him as soon as she got in tonight, although that promised to be late, the way things were going. Leaving Ryan at all would be a wrench, but Friday was only four days away, and she did have a lot of organising to do.

'I don't think anyone,' she said huskily, 'could feel happier than I do right now!'

'Want to bet?' asked the man she loved, coming back to life again. 'Prepare to be ravaged, woman!'

Ravished was a better word, came the thought as the sensual, knowledgeable mouth claimed hers. In the very finest sense, of course.

# PENNY JORDAN

**Sins and infidelities...**
**Dreams and obsessions...**
**Shattering secrets**
**unfold in...**

# THE HIDDEN YEARS

SAGE — stunning, sensual and
vibrant, she spent a lifetime
distancing herself from a past too
painful to confront... the mother
who seemed to hold her at bay,
the father who resented her and
the heartache of unfulfilled love.
To the world, Sage was
independent and invulnerable—
but it was a mask she cultivated to
hide a desperation she herself
couldn't quite understand...
until an unforeseen turn of events
drew her into the discovery of the
hidden years, finally allowing
Sage to open her heart to a
passion denied for so long.

**The Hidden Years**—a compelling novel of truth and passion
that will unlock the heart and soul of every woman.

AVAILABLE IN OCTOBER!
Watch for your opportunity to complete your Penny Jordan set.
POWER PLAY and SILVER will also be available in October.

---

HIDDEN

This October, Harlequin offers you a second
two-in-one collection of romances

# A SPECIAL SOMETHING

# THE FOREVER INSTINCT

by the award-winning author,

Barbara Delinsky

Now, two of Barbara Delinsky's most loved books are available together in this special edition that new and longtime fans will want to add to their bookshelves.

Let Barbara Delinsky double your reading pleasure with her memorable love stories, A SPECIAL SOMETHING and THE FOREVER INSTINCT.

Available wherever Harlequin books are sold. TWO-D

# HARLEQUIN

## Romance®

**This October,
travel to England with
Harlequin Romance
FIRST CLASS title #3155
TRAPPED
by Margaret Mayo**

"I'm my own boss now and I intend to stay that way."

Candra Drake loved her life of freedom on her narrow-boat
home and was determined to pursue her career as a company
secretary free from the influence of any domineering man.
Then enigmatic, arrogant Simeon Sterne breezed into her life,
forcing her to move and threatening a complete takeover of her
territory and her heart....

---